ENDORSEMENTS

"What a fresh and plucky voice Deines has—from her tart humor to her quirky and very real characters, every page is a delight. I will be recommending *A Dance with Hummingbirds* for years to come."

—**Lisa Tener**, Creator of the Award-Winning
Bring Your Book to Life® Program

"There's never a dull moment in the company of *Hummingbirds'* sassy and lovable heroine, Regina Richards. I couldn't get enough of her sarcastic wit."

—**Colette Freedman**, author of *The Affair* and *The Consequences*

"*A Dance with Hummingbirds* is an entertaining, expertly-paced, emotional and spiritual roller coaster. Helen Deines delivers a wholly original, quirky and deep debut that I literally couldn't stop reading."

—**Stuart Horwitz**, author of *Blueprint Your Bestseller: Organize and Revise any Manuscript with the Book Architecture Method*

A
Dance *with*
Hummingbirds

A
Dance *with*
Hummingbirds

A GIFT FROM THE OTHER SIDE

HELEN DEINES

A Regina Richards Novel

Berkeley Square Press

For Erwin, in loving memory

The hummingbird teaches us to transcend time, to recognize that what has happened in the past and what might happen in the future is not nearly as important as what we are experiencing now. It teaches us to hover in the moment, to appreciate its sweetness.

— Constance Barrett Sohodski

Nobody cares if you can't dance well. Just get up and dance.

— Martha Graham

CHAPTER ONE

I don't know when I first heard the whistling. It may have been days or months ago. But I remember exactly where I stood when I became aware of it.

It was a cold but beautiful Monday in March. The weather that new spring day promised to cooperate with my day's plans. Now all that was left was for *me* to cooperate with my day's plans.

I had just filled the bird feeders sprinkled around the back lawn. As I headed for the house, I could hear the frantic call of a blue jay letting his fellow feeders know that breakfast had arrived! I permitted myself one backward glance and espied a big old jay landing in the feeder and picking up two peanuts in his bill.

One of these days he is going to aim for three peanuts, I was thinking as I entered the kitchen, and it was then that I heard it.

Not just a random whistle, either, but that jaunty tune he favored. The one with no name. The one that had been a constant in our lives for thirty years.

But how was I hearing it now? The tune had left when he left. I looked around the kitchen as I fought back the tears. Without knowing what I was doing, I touched everything on the counters making sure things were in their proper place. I counted to fifty backward and tried to remember the Lord's Prayer in Polish. Anything to keep reality in check.

And then the music stopped. I know now what is meant by that old adage, "The silence was deafening." My heartbeat was as loud as the drums in Ravel's *Bolero*. Suddenly—out of pure defiance—I started to laugh.

Wasn't it just a few months ago I had shouted out to the world, "I am so lonely and scared! Can't someone give me a si_____ __ _____ __ _____ _____?"

ne. We were wa___ _____ ____ ____ ____ ____ wn's campus on t__ ____ ____ ____ ____ ____ ____ /eekend, and both ____ ____ ____ ____ ____ ____ lliott had on his c___ ____ ____ ____ ____ ____ -not to date myse__ ____ ____ ____ ____ ____ m from all over t__ ____ ____ ____ ____ ____ g our way back home after dinner ____ ____ ____ desire to watch a small boat make its way up the river.

Then he started to whistle.

"What's the name of that?" I asked.

"Um . . . I don't really know," he said. "For some reason I think it has a 'nightingale' in the title. I've been whistling it a long time."

Months later, and after a lot of research (everything related to our relationship seemed so *urgent* then), I found out the name of the tune. It was a song from the 1940s called "A Nightingale Sings in Berkeley Square." I remember how thrilled I was when I presented this information to Elliott, and I remember how stunned I was when he seemed sad about my news. That was not something I expected. And then we never talked about it again.

"Do you hear yourself whistle?" I had asked Elliott the first time I had heard him "perform."

He looked at me in surprise. And then with a chuckle he said, "Now that you mention it, I'm really not aware of it."

"I guess it's like that tree falling in the forest thing," I said, with only a dim idea of what the hell I was even talking about.

It didn't matter. We both laughed. In those days we laughed at everything, taking in the glorious scenes that unfolded before us, so comfortable in each other's company, so relaxed.

He ran his fingers through my red hair, looked into my eyes, and simply said, "You make me so happy."

I felt a small hole open in my heart, and then I felt his love creep in.

Now in the kitchen, I felt weak and sat down, trying to rationalize the whole thing away. What was happening with my head? Did I miss him so much that I willed myself into hearing things? The sound of two blue jays fighting in the yard woke me from my reverie, and I knew my day had to officially begin.

As I ran out the door—late, as usual—I remembered I needed to feed my cat, Maggie. Groaning, I turned back and reentered the house with only seconds to shut off the alarm.

My cat sat on the counter looking sage and wise. *You forgot to feed me again. What am I going to do with you?* she seemed to say to me.

Maggie is my sixteen-year-old cat. Truth be told, she was Elliott's cat more than she was mine. Without so much as a minute's worth of discussion on the pros and cons of owning a pet, I came home from work to meet the newest member of our family: a six-week-old calico kitten Elliott had decided to adopt from the pound. Not a wink of sleep was had for the next six weeks, or at least that was what it felt like as Maggie made it her mission to get familiar with every nook and cranny in the house. And when she wasn't doing that, she was using our bed as a trampoline.

Maggie quickly evolved into her role as Elliott's cat. She was always at his side, whether he was watching TV in the family room or hitting golf balls in the backyard. Her need to follow him so closely had even earned her a nickname from the neighbors: the puppy cat, they called her. Strange what you remember.

When he got sick and was hospitalized she withdrew to his side of the bed, only getting off to eat and drink in tiny amounts. I wondered if I was not going to have two losses to bear.

That morning in March when the phone rang and it was the hospital calling to say Elliott had died, I looked over at her and said, "Well, Maggs, I guess we are widows now."

I really think she understood the meaning of my words, because we stayed on that bed for hours in our own world of grief and sadness.

But the very next day Maggie was up with me and going about her cat duties and responsibilities. I truly believe on that night Maggie decided to live. Lying around waiting for the end was not what Elliott would do. And if she wasn't going to do it, I wasn't going to do it either.

As I opened the can of Fancy Feast, the most expensive can of cat food out there, thank you very much . . . I heard it again.

His whistle.

But what really shook me this time was the cat. Maggie was looking over the counter, her ears back and a grin on her face. She heard it, too.

I don't know who got into the dining room first, but that was where the sound was coming from. The dining room was never my favorite room in the home. For whatever reason, Elliott had opted to keep his parents' furniture.

It was mission oak, heavy wood with a singular lack of flair. The lines were straight and hard and it was plain old uncomfortable to sit in, to boot. The only silver lining here was that none of our dinner guests ever opted to linger in this room.

I did not know what to expect. Would I see him or part of him?

But there was no one in the room. The whistling had stopped again. Had we really even heard it? One look at Maggie assured me we had.

I had a strange feeling this was not the end of it.

My cell phone rang. Where the heck was my cell? Running to the kitchen I willed myself to calm down and simply follow the ringing.

Ah ha! It was in the cat food drawer. I never would have looked for it in there.

"Hello, hello," a voice said breathlessly on the other end of the phone. "Regina, where are you?"

I recognized the very low, yet familiar voice of my secretary, Diane. Diane had been with me for ten years. When I hired her she told me straight out that she would be moving on to other opportunities—I admired her directness—but that she would remain in my employ for at least a year so as to be worth the time I spent training her. At her last evaluation I had reminded her of that conversation.

She simply laughed. "Yeah, right?! Like I can go work for a normal person now?"

I was still unclear whether or not to be offended by that statement.

"They are both here and sitting down . . . and I can tell the small talk is winding to a close . . . pretty soon they're going to be demanding to know where you are, and I will have run out of things to say."

"What are you even talking about, Diane?"

"Your ten A.M. meeting with Carol and Dr. Piffs? That's what I'm talking about! To discuss the complaint Mrs. Staples's daughter made yesterday?"

"Oh, shit! I totally forgot about that. Wait—don't tell them that! Tell them I'm on my way, I just need to feed the cat."

I hung up on Diane and grabbed my keys, starting to leave for the second time that morning.

And then the radio began to play.

Maybe I needed a rest. Maybe I had gone back to work too soon. They told me that a loss like mine would . . .

Then the radio went silent.

A kiss to the cat and I was off.

CHAPTER TWO

My social service agency was not in the best part of town. The area where it was located had been a very affluent Jewish neighborhood: the large, brick, multi-family apartments had once been the homes of single families. The now-boarded-up and desolated temples had been the center of all things Jewish, but then they had discovered the suburbs—leaving in their wake the Irish with their towering churches and small shops, bakeries, and meat and produce depots that lined the great boulevard. And, of course, the bars. For every respectable store there was a drinking establishment, seemingly in a one-to-one ratio.

In recent years, the Irish too had begun to relocate, countered by an influx of Latino and African-American families. For one golden moment, everything seemed to be going on at once; everyone seemed to coexist reasonably, and the street had a life of its own. The fish man sold his smelly wares from a truck parked half on the sidewalk, the carpet man always had a sale going on, and every conceivable music sound could be heard, and I do mean *heard*, from passing autos. I felt more than a little out of place in my treasured Mercedes SUV, a gift from Elliott when his art gallery really started to take off.

Parking was impossible, and today it was no different. I pulled my car up in front of Barbara's Restaurant and tossed my keys to one of the waiters who would park it for me. I pretended not to know the Mercedes would be taken for a long, long journey before it was eventually parked somewhere nearby.

My office has been many things over the years. Once, it housed a small factory that cut carpet. In the fifties, it was a union hall, and in the early eighties, it had become a collective market. On humid days, you would swear you could still smell all of these previous incarnations mingling together: frayed carpet ends and spilled beer and deli meats. Or at least I could.

Today, the building houses a social service agency whose mission is to assist the elderly in our city to live in their homes independently and safely. That's our official task, at least. But we do a lot more than what is printed on our mission statement.

I quickly dodged into my office and dropped my bags onto the desk, not even flinching when the bags spilled several file folders onto the floor.

Diane handed me a cup of coffee as I prepared to do battle.

My plan was to stroll into the conference room and give the impression to those folks already assembled that not only had I been at work on time—I had actually arrived *early*. The reason for my tardiness was that I had been interrupted by an extremely important phone call.

As I sat down in my chair, I really thought I had carried it off. That is until I looked up at my supervisor, Carol, and her glare. It was the glare.

Carol's glare is legendary. So is the fact that her brain works in a kind of overdrive that must imply superior intelligence. When Carol encounters a problem she attacks it from all different angles at the same time. Before the rest of us mere mortals can finish reading a case, she has the problem assessed and the plan devised and put in place.

A one-woman think tank. Some days you can almost see her head spin as she debates herself.

She also has a language defect. She uses the word "fuck" as a noun, verb, and adjective. And Carol is never shy from using it anywhere, or with anyone.

For example: "What the fuck is this fuck?"

"I'm sorry," I responded.

"The fuck!" Carol said.

I should mention that Carol is also my mentor. As she drags me back to the conference room, she reminds me of the reason for our now-delayed meeting: We are discussing a difficult case with our resident psychiatrist, Roberta Piffs.

Elizabeth Staples. I have been having a very hard time wrapping my head around this case. Mrs. Staples is eighty-something and lives by herself in a big, old house in an affluent part of the city.

Our referral has come from Mrs. Staples's daughter, Paula, who lives in Boston. She had heard from her mother's clergy that her mother had become increasingly frail and had started to have memory issues. But here's the catch—Paula is adamant that she does not want her mother to know she is involved.

Which makes things pretty tricky. I've been to see Mrs. Staples twice but each time she threatened to call the police on me for trespassing. A reasonable perspective, given that she has no idea who I am or what I might be doing there.

Paula has since complained to Carol about my lack of progress, and we have gathered to discuss what I am doing wrong. Great; I'm up to speed.

To my utter amazement Carol lets Dr. P. take the lead. I start to protest but receive the glare, so I sit back in my chair.

"Let's try a little role-playing," Piffs says to the assembled group of social workers, who all simultaneously let out a groan. She glances around the room to see who she might torture. Pulling up one of my new hires, Alicia, Dr. P. announces that Alicia will be the client, and Piffs, naturally, will be me.

Ten minutes go by. Piffs struggles to make inroads into the client's psyche. None of her probing questions (read: psychobabble) has elicited one word from Alicia (as Mrs. Staples). Good girl, Alicia. Lunch is on me today.

Twenty minutes later, Piffs has lost everyone in the room. Laptops are open and phones are being used by all.

My gaze is centered on the one painting in the room. God, it's awful. Who paints apples and oranges in a blue fiesta bowl? There are other things that don't move in this world, you know. I resist the impulse to get up and see if it's signed.

Someone gently clearing their throat brings me back to the room.

Dr. Piffs is bordering on hysteria. Carol is bordering on a language malfunction, and she does not disappoint.

"You are all fucking morons!"

To this Piffs answers, "Oh!" as if she is unclear if Carol means to include her in that group, perhaps first and foremost, even. As Piffs backs out of the conference room, for a millisecond I even feel bad for her.

Carol's rage is turned on the rest of the group. "Have we wasted enough of each other's time today, waiting for everyone to wake the fuck up?"

It is unclear if this is a question that necessitates a reply. My kids are out the door within seconds, all considering themselves free and with the good fortune of having their heads still on.

"And shut the fucking door!"

Once again, I look over at the hideous painting. "Who do you think painted that monster?"

"My mother," comes the reply from Carol.

"Well, that's awkward."

"Yes," she says, then adds somewhat cryptically, "especially given the circumstances."

"Did she really paint that?"

"Of course not."

Now I can relax. Carol's humor bodes very well for my situation. Over the years I've developed my CAM (Carol Anger Meter). It rates her anger from 10 percent to 99 percent. One hundred percent has never knowingly been reached.

The use of humor means we are somewhere between 10 percent to 30 percent—"a walk in the park," I label this. Whatever infringement has set her off is minor and will likely subside in a matter of moments—certainly never making it into any employee's file.

More noteworthy is 30 percent to 60 percent. In those cases, the issue is "discussed" in a one-sided conversation between Carol and the penitent. Not good, but not the end of the world, either.

To reach 60 percent to 85 percent, you have to do something like ask for a Friday off in the summer before a long weekend, have your request denied, and then call in sick anyway. Uh-oh.

The only time I ever saw a reading over 85 percent was when an employee in the office was accused of tapping into the bank account of an elderly client to the tune of $5,000. Carol blew into the office at hurricane-wind speeds and fired the individual while simultaneously excoriating him of any sense of self-worth. She never mentioned his name again. And neither did we.

"You were late again this morning."

Seems like a reasonable thing for her to say. I'm not sure I love the use of "again," though. I'd put her at about 20 percent.

"Yup. But wait till I tell you why."

Carol turns in her chair, and I can see the glare has softened. A little bit of my mentor has joined my supervisor.

"It best be a doozy."

"Oh, but it is!"

Suddenly, I didn't want to tell Carol about the whistling. ~~I didn't want to tell anyone.~~ I worried ~~that perhaps if I was~~ to share my experience with someone, maybe that someone ~~would have a very rational reason~~ for what happened in my home this morning. And that would put an end to . . . Put an ~~end to *what*, exactly? What was~~ I hoping for?

Carol shifted in her seat as if to say "I'm waiting."

"I heard the whistling again. And the radio came on on its own."

"Do you still have the Bose?"

"The Bose. What the hell does that have to do with anything?"

"Nothing. But it's keeping me from thinking what I'm really feeling."

Leaving her chair, Carol strolled over to the one window we had in the conference room. My mentor was now in total control, having relegated my supervisor to another place. For a few seconds as she looked at me, she seemed sad, just terribly sad.

"You've been through a lot over the past few months. You are aware, aren't you, that not many people thought you were going to come out of this in a healthy way? I always felt you'd struggle a bit but that you'd get over it. Maybe I was wrong."

Carol sat back down and looked at me simply.

"Maybe you're overtired. Maybe you came back to work too soon. On the other hand, maybe you're just a nut."

"Is that what we call people now? What is that short for, nut, nutcase? Is that my diagnosis?"

"I'm not sure. I'll ask Piffs when she decides to start talking to me again."

And then we both started to laugh and laugh a lot. And the laughter was heard throughout the office, causing some folks to leave their desks to verify what they were hearing. It had been a long time since anyone remembered hearing the sound of laughter coming from the end of the hall.

I went back to my office to answer phone messages. Eleven yellow notes filled one side of the desk; those were the calls that needed to be answered yesterday. Fifteen similar yellow missives sat awaiting attention on the other side of the desk. Those calls were from today. I had every intention of jumping in and answering every call, but a picture of Elliott and me took importance.

We were in Ocho Rios in Jamaica. It seemed like a hundred years ago, but the date on the photograph verified it was taken just six years ago. Elliott was radiant looking. So healthy. No sign of what was coming his way.

And me? I gazed out at the camera, so smug in my belief that this good life was never going to end.

I return to my phone messages and watched myself pick up the phone twice and each time put it back down. I know when I've lost the battle. Looking down at all of the unanswered calls and noticing my phone alerting me to more incoming calls, I decide just to listen to my gut and attempt another visit to Mrs. Staples. The rest of this work would still be there when I got back in the afternoon—that was the good old trusty thing about work.

As luck would have it, my Mercedes pulled up in front of my office just as I opened the front door to my office building. Perfect timing.

As the driver leaned over to hand me the keys, I realized I didn't recognize him.

"You new?" I asked.

"Ma'am?"

"Are you a new waiter at Barbara's?"

Without meeting my look, the young man seemed to stare at the ground as he contemplated his answer.

"Ah, yeah, I'm new."

Not for the first time did I question my choice of valet service.

Driving across town, my thoughts circled around Mrs. Staples. I didn't fully understand why this case was taking on such a significant meaning. It certainly was not the first time I had been rebuffed by an elder. And I knew it would not be my last. Perhaps it was because Piffs was involved . . .

Mrs. Staples, Mrs. E. Staples, Mrs. Eleanor Staples. I wonder what she called herself. What did her friends call her? Did she have friends . . . ?

She was in her eighties and lived alone. She had been married to a physician whom Paula described as the "last of the country docs" still making house calls into his eighties. . .

Paula was an only child who described herself as being very close to her father when she was a child, but less close as an adult. She did state that she always felt her mother had resented the relationship between father and daughter . . .

This was brought home to Paula when she called home one year to extend birthday wishes to her dad. Her mother informed her that her father had died and been privately waked and buried. This was the first Paula had heard of her father's passing.

Well, there was clearly something wrong with that! Perhaps an early case of dementia . . .

Arriving at Mrs. Staples's home, I decided to hang back a bit and observe.

Even though the home was in an affluent area, it was beginning to look a little seedy. The front steps needed work, and a couple dozen cans of paint would help. The house itself was a large colonial that sat up on a hill. Except for a number of old and stately oak trees, there was no landscaping to speak of, no lush grass or ornamental shrubs or seasonal flower beds. Just oak trees. It gave the house a tired look.

Or maybe it was just me. Climbing up to the veranda, I took in the simplicity of the wood work. What you couldn't note from the street was the beauty of the design. I couldn't help but think what a joy it would be to sit out here with a glass of wine and watch the world go by.

The time had come. I rang the doorbell and listened to it as it echoed within the walls. It was a safe house, if not a happy house.

The door opened a crack, and I heard Mrs. Staples mutter, "Not you again."

"Yup, it's me, and I need ten minutes of your time," I said in my best official-sounding voice.

"It's March 6, 2011, and it is a Monday."

"What did you say?"

From behind the heavy door, Mrs. Staples said, "Well, that is what you were going to eventually ask me, is it not?"

"I guess, but . . ."

My amazement that she knew I was there to investigate her mental state turned from awe to anger as I recalled Piffs's tragic attempt at role-play earlier in the day.

"Look, Mrs. Staples. You don't want me here. I get it. But I have to see you, and yes, I have to ask you the day and date. And I have to ask you a bunch of other things. I—just like you—would really like to get this over with sooner rather than later. You should see the piles of messages on my desk at my office of *people who want to talk to me*. But in the meantime, I'm just going to sit on your porch until you come out. And if you don't come out today I'll be back tomorrow. And if you don't come out . . . Are you getting where I'm going with this?"

"This is harassment. I shall call the police."

"Please do. And while you're on the line with them make sure they send the proper unit, the officers who can escort me into your house to do a wellness check on you."

My heart was racing. I wondered again at what mysterious energy seemed to be taking over this case. I never ever remembered acting in such an outlandish manner toward an elder. I certainly didn't blame Mrs. Staples for slamming the door in my face.

I now faced the grim notion of an impasse, of sitting on her veranda for the rest of the day, or perhaps all month—maybe even for years! I must be losing my mind. This thought brought a grin as I could not help but think that that idea had come up a lot today.

A few minutes passed, and, to my amazement, the front door opened and Mrs. Staples came out onto her veranda.

She picked an old rocker and sat directly opposite from me.

There she gently rocked, and I watched.

CHAPTER THREE

Mrs. Staples and I continued sitting on her veranda in a silence that was startling. It did, however, afford me the opportunity to cast a few sidelong glances at the woman. She clearly didn't look her age of eighty-five. Her hair was white, almost a pure white, with no gray at all. Had she ever been gray, or had her hair gone white overnight? *White hair certainly makes a woman look younger than gray hair,* I noted to myself for my own purposes in the upcoming decades.

Mrs. Staples's skin was without lines or wrinkles. It was as if she never had a worry in her life. She certainly had never spent much time out in the sun. The style of her royal blue and white silk dress was outdated, yet it emanated a sense of royalty. I could almost picture Queen Elizabeth on her rocker greeting her guests in similar attire.

Mrs. Staples kept her hands firmly clasped in her lap. She wore a gold wedding ring and a watch that seemed out of place on her. My attention zeroed in on that watch. Something about it just did not match with the entire ladylike picture that made up Mrs. Staples . . . then it hit me. Of course—it was not something an eighty-five-year-old lady would wear because it was a man's watch. Her husband's?

As I sat staring at her hands and that watch, Mrs. Staples must have felt my stare, because she pulled them farther into her lap. On the watch's retreat, I glimpsed some kind of medallion connected to the watch band at the top: the size of a dime and painted blue. It was unusual and familiar at the same time.

I decided it was time to break the silence. "I like your watch. Very different."

Silence.

"Very peaceful out here . . . very peaceful. One almost forgets that the city is just around the corner!"

Silence.

Suddenly, Mrs. S. stopped her gentle rocking.

"Please tell me why you are here. Someone must have given you my name. And *please* do not say it was an anonymous caller, because I will not believe it."

As I sat there trying to figure out how to answer that, she turned and said in a voice that was both authoritarian and bold:

"Well, are you going to tell me?"

"You won't like the answer."

"Try me."

"It was an anonymous caller."

Mrs. Staples glared at me. "You are totally correct in that perception. I do not like it, nor do I believe it."

I was desperate to continue our fledgling little conversation, but as I struggled to think of what to say next, Mrs. S. beat me to it.

"So what exactly is the purpose of this so-called visit?"

"My job is to inform older adults of services they may be eligible for, in order for the community to serve them best."

Okay, so maybe repeating a canned mission statement was not the wisest choice. . .

"What rot!" Mrs. S. responded forcefully. "I'm not eligible for welfare."

"It's not welfare *per se*. Some of the services are state-supported," I added, as if that made a difference. "All state residents are eligible for them."

"Like a beach pass or free bus rides?" she snorted derisively.

I was getting her angry, and usually that does not produce good results. I also began to recognize my own growing feelings of frustration. I'm usually very good in opening up dialogue with older folks, some even as stubborn as Mrs. Staples. But I was off my game; maybe the ridiculous role-playing with Piffs this morning had gotten in my head and made me start to doubt myself. . .

Mrs. Staples rescued me from my dark thoughts. "Why didn't you send me a pamphlet or let me know you wanted to visit?"

Mrs. Staples suddenly asked, "Was it my daughter, Paula?" I remained non-committed.

"Would you have responded?"

That was met with a glare that rivaled anything my supervisor Carol could have mustered.

"You know, you may be surprised, but some people actually *enjoy* my visits."

"That would indeed surprise me."

For a millisecond I thought I spied the start of a smile on her face. Then I decided it must have been my imagination.

"Well, I've got to go," I said as I started for the stairs. "Work to do, you know. People to help."

Mrs. Staples looked up, and surprise registered in her eyes.

"See you tomorrow?" I asked. "Same time, same place?"

I waited for her negative response, but none came.

Progress? Only when I was sitting in the Mercedes did I sneak a look back at the Staples home. Mrs. S. was gone, and the house looked quiet and untouched.

Lots of secrets there, lots of secrets.

CHAPTER FOUR

That tale I had told Mrs. Staples about going back to work that afternoon was just that. Today had been too long already, and it needed to end.

I drove the rest of the way home on autopilot with thoughts of a glass of wine and a good crime show the only things on my mind. When I turned into my driveway, I saw that I had left my garage door open. With all of the conflicting efforts I had made to leave this morning, I was not entirely surprised. What did surprise me was the fact that as I pulled up closer, the door started to come down . . . without my having pushed the button.

I brought my car to a stop and got out for a peek, hoping none of my neighbors would see me standing there. It wouldn't really do for them to see me looking totally French-fried. As I started to approach the garage on foot, the door opened up once again, that grinding of metal on metal revealing the inside of a garage, which now looked to me as if it were possessed.

"Oh, fuck!"

I called Pete and waited inside my car for an hour for him to get to my home. Pete is my "handyman." He prefers "contractor."

"Hey, girlfriend. What's up?" Pete was dressed in his usual uniform of jeans and a sweatshirt, with a somewhat filthy baseball hat on his head.

"I told you. The garage door keeps opening and closing on its own."

With the look of male superiority reserved for mechanical things, Pete said: "That's impossible."

And the door opened up.

"How did you do that?" he said, backing away from the door.

"I didn't," I said as the door closed.

"Use the thinger to see if it works."

"The thinger? Really, Pete? This is why you're a handyman."

"The garage-door opener."

Returning to the Mercedes I grabbed the opener/thinger and pressed it several times. Nothing happened. I shook it unmercifully as Pete watched in amusement.

"Shaking it, huh. That helping?"

The shaking didn't help.

"I'll look into the motor," Pete said.

I have always been leery of small men on ladders, so I chose to look away. I'm not sure that's a rational fear, but there you have it.

Suddenly, smoke was everywhere. It was coming from the motor box, a black, foul-smelling smoke. Pete managed to disconnect the motor, and the smoke stopped.

"Wow!" we said in unison.

As we stared at the burnt-out motor, it was Pete who finally said, "There is no question as to whether there was going to be a fire in this thing. The only question was *when* was there going to be a fire in this thing."

Several minutes passed as we cleaned out the garage. Suddenly a thought entered my head that made me stop and feel very afraid.

"Do you smell anything?"

"Yeah. Smoke." Pete's eyes narrowed. "Actually, I do, like a cologne?"

The distinct and heavy smell of cologne filled the garage. "Pete, are you wearing any cologne?"

"I prefer *eau du cigarette*." He seemed to think that was quite amusing.

It was Bay Rum. There was no mistaking it, the same Bay Rum Elliott began to use when his cancer took hold. Trying to mask the smell of death.

And we both smelled it now.

"What's going on?" Pete said.

"Pete, I think Elliott is here. Right here in the garage."

Whether it was from relief at finally saying it out loud or just the look on Pete's face, I started to laugh, and Pete laughed, too.

But when the garage door suddenly started to close again without any power source, we both stopped laughing.

Pete simply said, "I'll call the garage-door guy."

CHAPTER FIVE

As I sat on the deck with a glass of wine, I mulled over what the garage-door person told us about my wayward door.

"Well, that just can't happen!"

That was reassuring.

"I'll need for you to call the office tomorrow to give them a credit card number . . ." the garage-door guy was saying—at least he was up to speed with getting money for his company, his manager ought to be proud—"excuse me, ma'am, but are you even listening to me?"

"I am! Indeed. Now, may I ask you a question?"

"Do you mind if I sit down a minute?" Mr. Garage-Door Guy asked. "I've been on my feet all day."

He joined Pete on the outdoor double recliner, and Pete passed him a beer.

After he had taken a few swigs, I asked: "Are you sure a door simply can't go up and down on its own?"

It was here that I noted Garage-Door Guy was looking at me strangely.

"Huh, yeah, sure . . ." He looked like he wanted to say more. I waited. "Ma'am, I've been a certified door expert for more than fifteen years. You wouldn't believe some of the crazy things that garage doors can do. But in my professional opinion, those crazy things are usually somehow related to crazy people."

Pete jumped in, "Dude, what's your point? There's nobody crazy here. . ."

"My point—*dude*—is that I saw your door open and close on its own twice. You were nowhere near it, and the lady was nowhere near it. It seemed to take on a life of its own. . ."

"What the hell does that mean, 'a life of its own'?"

"Pardon me, ma'am. The door did open, and it did close . . . but, ma'am, it wasn't plugged in!"

This observation left all three of us in a reflective silence. Reality was shifting ever so slightly; I was sitting there wondering, since when was having a power source such a big deal!

"Yeah, I guess I get your point," I said.

"Maybe you should think about having it exorcised or something?"

I glared at Garage-Door Guy, who suddenly decided he didn't need the rest of his beer.

"Well, I best be getting back. . ."

Picking up his papers, he practically ran off the deck.

"Hey!" I called after him. "Aren't you going to show me how to use the new remote?"

"Ma'am," he called back, "I left the instructions—here's hoping they apply!" And with that he made a beeline for his truck.

"Well, you have a knack for making new friends," Pete said from his spot on the outdoor couch.

"I get it from you!" I said. "Hey, you want to see what this new baby can do?"

I pointed toward the garage with the recently installed opener, then turned it over in my hands. This thing was like the Cadillac of remotes. . . How much were they going to ding me for tomorrow morning when I called the garage-door installer's office?

Pete was looking at me expectantly. I raised the remote again and pointed it at the garage. But I swear I didn't press anything when the door started going up on its own.

"That was me!" the Garage-Door Guy called from behind the hedges, coming back down the driveway. "That was me. I forgot to give you the extra remote."

He handed it to me with a sheepish grin. "Just having a little fun's all."

I thought I had had enough fun for one night after my meeting with Piffs, my encounter with Mrs. S., and now this. Even though it was only eight P.M., I decided the day was over for me and Maggie. She headed toward the bedroom, and I headed toward the bath.

In my reverie in the bath I could hear Maggie pacing over the covers, waiting impatiently.

"I'll be with you in fifteen minutes," I yelled to the cat.

After a soak, I felt slightly more empowered and slipped under the covers.

"Quite a day Miss M. . . . Quite a day."

She seemed to understand as she arched her body against my knee. "I think it might help if you purr just a little until I nod off. . . ." And she did, and so did I.

It was still dark outside when something woke me up.

I was in the process of convincing myself that the disturbances were in my mind, when I heard it again . . . music . . . maybe something by Christo? But I don't own any Christo music. The only time I hear that music is when I'm in the office, where everyone except me is a fan.

My plan was simple. Stay in bed and put the pillow over my head until the music stopped. Don't try to figure out where it was coming from, or what crazy neighbor was getting their Christo fix at this hour—just tune it out and go back to sleep.

Half an hour later, no sleep. More Christo. No cat—where had Maggie gotten to? I decided to search for her, and as I did, I came up with a new theory: *power surges.* Yes! Some sort of power surge was taking over my house . . . maybe the power surge had spread from the garage door opener to the Bose radio . . . A spontaneous, contagious power surge!

The memory of the unplugged door opener put a damper on that theory.

As I crept down the stairs, the music got louder. Upon entering the kitchen, I turned on all the lights. The entire room leapt out in colors of red, gold, and stainless steel. Abruptly, the music stopped. And the Bose shut off.

I stared at the Bose like it was a sleeping cobra. Hesitating, I approached the offending machine with caution. Only after pushing several buttons in random order did I turn the Bose back on.

I pressed the eject button, and the CD slipped out. Carole King's *Her Greatest Hits*. That was better than Christo any day.

Maybe my boss was right, maybe I had returned to work too soon. Maybe my mind was not quite right, you know, relatively speaking to where it had been before. Looking around the kitchen, I noticed nothing was out of place.

I decided not to return to bed and rationalized my decision by the fact that it was almost dawn. I needed to get up anyway, maybe—hey! Maybe today I wouldn't be late!

Deep down, of course, I knew I was just too scared to sleep. Running back upstairs I found a reasonably clean pair of jeans and a sweater to put on.

Making tea in the dawn light, I could almost feel the house breathe. I used to feel whole here. Taking my tea to the deck, I watched the sun come up. Looking over the wooded acres that make up my backyard, I remembered the first time I laid eyes on this patch of heaven.

We had been looking with a real estate agent when Elliott decided to come up to our favorite area to scout on his own for any new homes for sale. He found an empty lot with only a sign—the paint was literally still wet: FOR SALE BY OWNER.

I met him there an hour later. We walked the property, and it was perfect. Mature trees and wild shrubs covered the terrain. It even had a small brook and an ancient cemetery going back to before the Civil War.

We called the owner right then and there and bought the land the next day. We built our home together. Every decision was one we made jointly, from the design of the front of the house as it faced the road to the smallest of the appliances. Even the sweet pepperbush shrub that we had exactly one of, we had decided together to have only one and where it would go.

For some reason, this lone bush with its strange white flowers caused all of the pain to come rushing back. All of the happy times we had shared in this home were gone. It felt physical. How was I ever going to get over this? Would I get over it?

The despair was intense, and I could pinpoint the part of my heart where the grief seemed like it would never leave. I remembered the last time we spoke of his disease, both of us keenly aware that our time together was winding down.

We held hands and spoke of the inevitable. "I want to be cremated."

"I know."

"Do not let anyone talk you out of it."

"I won't."

"Bring my ashes home and toss them in the woods. Or better yet, just sprinkle them on these flowers right by the deck."

"Okay."

"You know, I'm not fully signed on to this reincarnation stuff you believe in. But if I do come back, I want to come back as one of our hummingbirds . . . So put my ashes near their feeder. That's where I want to be."

"For God's sake, why?" I asked.

Elliott stopped and looked down to his hands. He had trouble with emotion, especially talking about his emotions.

"I've thought about this for a long time. Sitting out here and watching the hummingbirds over the years has given me a real sense of peace. And yet I am in awe of them as well . . .

"They fly up here the same time every year from halfway around the world, and apparently they never get lost. They fly in ways that defy logic—backward and even upside down—and they look so graceful doing it. Like a mob of ballerinas!"

At that I had to laugh, you know, this being Rhode Island and all.

"So you want to come back in the mob?"

"No, I want to come back to do the one thing we never did together, and I think the hummingbirds can help me here."

Suddenly Elliott looked more confident than he had since the conversation had started.

Grabbing my hand he said, "I want to come back and dance with you, Regina! I want to waltz around a ballroom with music played by a fifteen-piece band. I want to wear a tuxedo and maybe even special shoes, you know, the ones that make you seem to glide over the floor. I want you to wear a ball gown and heels, and I want to hold you and lead you in a waltz—a waltz that belongs to us, Regina, like we never got to this time around. I want to come back to dance with you!"

I sat in amazement staring at Elliott. In all of the almost thirty years we had been together, I had never seen him more passionate.

Fighting back tears, I simply said, "How will the hummingbirds make this happen?"

"If I come back . . . no, *when* I come back, I know those hummingbirds are going to make it happen. I don't know how, but when I return they will be right here waiting for me."

That conversation had happened so long ago, but now it seemed as if it had just been yesterday. For some reason, it brought me peace.

I sat with my tea for a little bit longer. I heard the sounds of the neighborhood waking up: the jays telling each other to wake and start the day. The red squirrel peeked out from the deck, wary of his bigger cousin, bedecked in gray. In the distance, a front door opened and closed as someone retrieved their paper.

My reverie was broken when I realized that the sweater I was wearing was Elliott's. I had no idea how it got into my drawer; all of his clothes were in his dressing room neatly hanging and waiting for the day when I could finally get to the place to give them to charity.

Wouldn't you know it? I was going to be late again today.

CHAPTER SIX

At the office that day, I didn't even try to hide from Carol—instead, I walked right up to her.

"Do you guys have any Christo?"

Carol laughed, and in a moment I could see her expression change from miffed to bemused. "I thought you hated Christo."

"I'm doing some research."

"Oh," Carol said, taking a bite out of her chocolate chip cookie. "Yeah, I think there's one of his CDs in the player in the conference room. . . You were late again."

I had been saving this tactic for a while. Now, I nonchalantly slid into it. . .

"Hey, instead of talking about why I'm late all the time, why don't we talk about why you are always early? Hmmm?"

Carol covered her mouth with her hand, either to hide a smile or her chewing, I couldn't be sure which.

"I get here early because I want to procure a parking spot in the lot, in order to avoid having to rely on ex-cons to park my car."

"They're not ex-cons," I said with a lot of false confidence.

"Ah, yes they are. What do you think they mean when they tell you they are going south for a few months?"

This was not looking favorable for me. "That they're going to Florida?"

"No, incorrect. They are going south to Cranston, the home of the state prison."

"Ohhhh. You've been dying to share that with me, haven't you?"

Carol pointed with her full mouth toward my desk, indicating our audience was over.

On the way toward my office, my secretary, Diane, perked her head up. "So what's the next move, maybe a séance?"

"First, I'm going to listen to some Christo," I said in a voice I felt would confirm our working relationship of boss versus non-boss.

It did not work.

"Well, if you want to borrow my Ouija board over the weekend, just let me know," Diane remarked.

A few minutes later, she was back at my door.

"Pearl is here."

We work with a lot of people. I just needed a minute. . .

"Pearl! How'd she get here? What does she want?"

Pearl was a client of mine who was in her eighties. She was married to Leo who was recently hospitalized with a severe stroke. Pearl wanted to take him home to care for him. Everyone involved: doctors, physical therapists, nurses, even her family members thought that was a really bad idea. A real potential disaster even. I'd been trying to get her to change her mind and accept a nursing home placement for Leo, but as of that moment, I'd not made any inroads.

Hustling out to the reception area, I spied Pearl in all her glory. Pearl was a rather short, somewhat large lady. She was dressed in the way that people dress when they haven't been around others very often for a while . . . what she was wearing could be described as a potato sack with a belt. Her hair was unkempt, and her skin color was tomato red. I sensed a problem, and I didn't really want to deal with this, but I had no choice when she came rushing at me. For a millisecond I thought she was going to take me down, like a rogue elephant.

"Pearl, how did you get here?"

"I took a taxi."

"You paid for a taxi?" That in itself stunned me. Pearl is not known for her largesse.

"Well, no, I didn't exactly pay for it. One of those nice, young men hanging outside your building offered to pay."

I was totally stupefied. "Are you talking about the waiters outside the restaurant?"

"Regina, dear, I don't think they're real waiters," she said, shaking a finger in my face.

Apparently my power of observation was lacking in the criminal recognition arena.

"So how did you get them to pay?"

"I told them I was your mother."

I stared at her. "You told them you were my mother."

"Sure, but you favored your father's side."

I led Pearl back to my office and motioned for her to sit down in the more uncomfortable chair of the two. I wasn't giving away any more favors today.

"So, Pearl. What's up?"

"I had to see you! I have good news. Leo wants to come home."

I asked Diane to get us some coffee, hoping that would give me a few additional minutes before I spoke.

"Okay, Pearl. And how do you know this?"

"He told me."

"Oh . . . I see." I had to proceed here with caution—didn't want this to be a case of the pot calling the kettle black.

"Pearl, he is in a coma. A very deep coma. Imagine there are gradations of coma, Pearl. The doctors have likened this one to death."

Looking very sure of herself, Pearl stated: "I am aware of what the doctors have said, but Regina, you have to believe me! He woke up yesterday and told me he wanted to come home."

"In just those words?"

"Yes," she said, with a little less bravado this time.

I looked at her with a skeptical glance, and she retreated a bit.

"Well, no . . . but I know he wants to come home. There don't have to be words between married people. We know what our partner wants or needs without words."

I closed my eyes. Life was indeed complicated.

"People who are married for a long time can feel special things," Pearl went on.

This was true. Or thought they did . . .

"Okay. Pearl, do you think Leo could tell me he wants to go home?"

"I think so. Yes, I do believe he could."

"Pearl, I can't promise you anything, but here is the plan. You and I are going to visit with Leo and ask him if he wants to come home, and if he can convince me he does, then I'll see what I can do."

"I knew you would help me."

"But, on the other hand, if Leo can't tell me his wishes, then we drop this once and for all and begin to look for a nursing home."

"It's a deal!"

During our conversation, Pearl had seemed to metamorphosize right in her chair. The redness of her skin had changed to a glow. Even the potato sack/dress began to have class.

I thought I recognized what this was, as guilty as I had been of it lately. It was hope.

As we were walking out, Carol met us in the foyer. "How did she get here?" she whispered loudly.

"A taxi!" I whispered back.

"She paid for a taxi?"

"Let's not go there."

Ten minutes later, as we drove into the hospital garage, I remembered our unbreakable rule about transporting clients in our private vehicles.

"Pearl, let's let this ride be our little secret, okay?"

"Sure," she said.

"No, not just, 'Sure,' Pearl, but 'Yes, Regina, cross my heart and hope to die.'"

"Sure," she said again, and with that Pearl opened the door to my Mercedes SUV and fell out onto the pavement, hitting the ground with a *thwack*!

"Jesus, I am so screwed!" Shutting off the car, I swung my door open and ran over to examine the damage.

Pearl was sitting on the pavement. I didn't see any blood or bones sticking out. Her dress was disheveled and one shoe was off, but this was Pearl after all.

"I missed the step."

Great! She could talk so she probably didn't have a concussion.

"Do you hurt anywhere? Is anything broken?"

Pearl gingerly examined herself, checking her elbows, knees, and hips.

"No, nothing seems broken," she said, cautiously. "I landed on my tush."

My relief was instantaneous: "You hit your butt? Only your butt?" I was flooded with the notion that maybe I could survive this. Pearl had a huge butt!

Getting her up off the pavement was no easy feat, but somehow we managed to get her righted, fix her dress, and put her shoe back on.

"Can you walk?" I asked.

Using the car door as a prop, I watched in silence as she gingerly took a few steps.

My heart was racing, and I felt I was going to pass out myself when Pearl turned to me with a big smile on her face and said, "I'm just fine. Let's go see Leo."

It was then that I bowed my head to the god that looks after social workers that break all of the rules. He/She was going to be kind today, and I would live to break more rules tomorrow!

We made our way up to Leo's room. Poor Leo, looking so very frail and sickly. He lay in bed with tubing everywhere. He had IVs in both arms and a giant mask affixed to his nose and mouth. The sound of the room was that of a well-oiled machine with *shuss*ing noises and *click-clack*ing noises. There was a smell in the room, too. It was not a healthy smell.

A nurse followed us in and gently sat Pearl down.

"Pearl, Leo did not have a good night. He was very restless."

"Oh," says Pearl. "He'll sleep better when he is home. In his own bed."

The nurse stepped back with a quizzical look on her face and said, "No, Pearl, that isn't what we discussed yesterday. Taking Leo home is not an option. He needs too much care. And even if you had someone to help you with him it would be too hard on you, Pearl."

"Wait a second," I asked. If he is in a death-like coma . . . how is he acting very restlessly?"

"Involuntary movements," the nurse confided in me.

As I was trying to figure that one out, Pearl drew herself up to her full height. Looking at this woman, you would not believe that she had just recovered from a fall out of an SUV.

With her hands by her side, Pearl said, "That's why Regina is with me. She is going to help me take Leo home. Aren't you, Regina?"

Hearing my name as part of this unsanctioned care plan snapped me back into awareness.

"Sure, Pearl," I said. "Why don't you tell the charge nurse your plan for taking Leo home?"

"It's our plan, Regina."

The nurse leaned over and asked me, "And who are you, again?"

"She's my social worker," Pearl answered on my behalf, "and when Leo tells her he wants to go home, she is going to make all the arrangements."

I waved my hands horizontal to the ground away from each other over and over again, making the universal signal of 'No, this is no good, that's not what we're really talking about' behind Pearl's back. It did not seem to help the nurse understand my plight.

"You two stay right here. I'm going to page the doctors. I'm positive they are going to want to hear about this, too."

As the nurse left to call the doctor, I wondered if she would also ask the doc to refer me to a malpractice hearing.

Pearl took Leo's hand and in a voice that could only be described as delusional, Pearl sing-songed, "Leo, tell Regina you want to go home!"

What happened next fit neatly in with the whistling and the music and the garage door.

Leo opened his eyes and smiled at Pearl, and then slowly, very slowly, he reached up and grabbed Pearl's very ornate pendant and began to twist it. As Pearl commanded Leo to fill me in about his wishes, Leo took a two-handed grip on the jewelry and began twisting it and twisting it.

Pearl began to change color going from her usual red to very red. Leo continued to twist her necklace. I decided it was time to intervene when Pearl's breathing became labored. I mean, the man had a death grip on the chain, and he was not about to give it up. It was clear to me that Leo had a plan, but it was not to go home with Pearl. It was to send her home in a box!

I grabbed Leo's hands and tried to free his hold on the chain. After several long seconds, I still could not pry his hands loose. The chain was almost up to Pearl's chin, and Leo showed no signs of letting go. Pearl continued to talk with him, but her voice was now just a whisper.

When her breathing got downright labored, I decided I needed help.

The call bell was nowhere in sight. I had to get help now, so I let go of the chain and decided to get the attention of some nurses at the station next door. Mustering my most professional tone I yelled, "Help! Help! Leo is killing Pearl!"

At the station, several nurses and aides looked up but no one moved.

"Really, goddamnit!"—there went the professionalism out the window—"Help me, for fuck's sake! Leo is really trying to strangle Pearl!"

At some point, I'd have to talk to Carol about the effectiveness of obscenities. But maybe not using this story. Several nurses and attendants had now gotten the point and were running into the room.

"Code blue! Code blue!" rang out over the intercom, signaling a life-threatening event. Emergency staff with the crash cart flew into Leo's room and took a second to figure out who needed the emergency attention.

What seemed like a minute was in reality forty-five minutes.

Pearl was escorted out of the room with a very nasty welt around her neck. Her coloration was awful, and her clothing was soiled and torn.

What the heck had happened in that room?

I found her a chair and gently led her down into the seat. She grasped my hand in a vise-like grip, and in a very raspy voice said: "Leo has passed. But I still think he wanted to come home with me."

CHAPTER SEVEN

I work nine to five. With a job like mine, I think that's important. I don't cut corners . . . okay, maybe I get there at 9:12 sometimes, but then I stay until 5:15. I give it my all, and then, when the end of the day rolls around, I go home. Because otherwise? I could be thinking about the wacky and wonderful world of my clients 24/7.

After getting Pearl safely home, it was only 4:15 P.M., so I decided to end my day by sitting on Mrs. Staples's veranda. I wasn't really sure who needed it more. She didn't seem surprised to see me. We sat quietly for a few minutes, and then I asked her if she wanted to hear about my day.

Mrs. S. looked away, and I barely heard her as she said, "Yes."

I told her about Christo, which led to discussing the whistling, which led to my chronically-a-little-bit-lateness, which led to my ex-con valet people, which led to the saga of Pearl and Leo. It sounded pretty crazy to me, but Mrs S. was turning out to be a skilled conversationalist.

"Were they ever happily married?"

For a split-second, I thought she meant me.

"Pearl and Leo? I doubt it. I don't think he was happy, but I think she was. I think for the first time in her life, Pearl felt safe." It felt good to talk to someone. "Leo was overwhelmed. He left the house every day except Sundays at nine A.M. and walked the dog all day. Then he came home at three in the afternoon, had dinner, and went to bed."

"What did they do on Sunday?"

"On Sunday, he'd stay home until noon, when he left to walk the dog until three again."

"What was the dog's name?"

Here we go. You never know when the old folks are going to go down a strange road on ya. "The dog's name? I don't know."

"Well, you should find out."

"Why?"

"Won't it be to your benefit when you advertise to have the dog's name?"

I sat back in the outdoor wicker chair in a state of complete confusion. It had to be getting close to five o'clock. Time to wrap this day up.

"What will I be advertising for?"

"A dog walker. Someone is going to have to walk the dog. Pearl certainly doesn't sound like she's going to be the woman for the job."

I had to admit that was not something I had ever thought about. Here I was thinking I was humoring her, and once again, she was two steps ahead of me.

"So it would be a good thing to know the dog's name. I'm going in now. Feel free to stay, if you'd like."

"No, thank you. I think I'll go home, too." I picked up my pocketbook and straightened my shoes, which were always slipping.

"Regina? Are you fearful of what is happening around you?"

That was a good question. It deserved a good answer.

"I don't know what I feel."

"It may turn out you have a gift. A great gift." Mrs. S. turned and walked into the house.

CHAPTER EIGHT

For the next few weeks, relative calm reigned. Monday through Friday, nine to five, clients came and went. In the off hours, my house was mercifully, quiet.

Pearl decided to give Leo an over-the-top sendoff. A wake followed by a church funeral. The wake was attended by all of their friends who were still living, which made for about six people in all. One of whom came with her mandolin and serenaded us for an hour. It made Pearl very proud.

Maybe it was just my "stuff," but I was a little concerned about the lack of bodies at the wake, so I made attendance at the funeral mandatory for my staff. I managed to convince Carol to make an appearance, and even persuaded two of my ex-con valet parkers to attend the funeral. Both were reasonably confused to see my "mother" in the receiving line.

At the office, we did paperwork, scheduled visits—sometimes we even helped people. If they could be helped, if they weren't squatters, like the two sisters, Ann and Belle, who were referred to the agency for heating assistance. They told me they owned their house and were living on the first floor because the stairs were too much for them to handle. Only when we started working with another government agency who liaised with the natural gas company did we find out the sisters did not own the home at all; rather, it had been sold at auction for unpaid taxes.

One problem led to another. Take Milo, for example. When I visited with him in his house, things were reasonably messy but not overwhelming. Soon thereafter I found out that this was Milo's fourth home. The other three were filled to the rafters with stuff. Everything from old gas stoves to broken eyeglasses. One hundred and sixty-three pairs of broken eyeglasses in a single hallway. What do you do, except maybe call the television show *Hoarders*? Nine to five, I kept telling myself. Help who you can and learn how to live on your own again. That's somebody you can help: yourself. My days were slipping by quickly, and summer was fast approaching. Maybe it was time to paint the house or walk the property with a gardener and add a few new trees. Maybe it was time to relinquish Elliott's ashes.

It was his wish to have his cremated remains spread in the gardens he loved so much and had spent so much time tending.

Maggie and I decided on a spot very close to the woods. It was peaceful and quiet, and I was already planning a separate garden there to recognize him. The cat followed me down a certain path for a bit, then veered off into the woods. I expected she had her own way planned to say goodbye to her best friend.

I had just finished emptying the urn and was sitting on the deck when something moving out of the woods caught my attention.

It was Maggie. No longer the orange and black cat but now a gray cat, gray from her whiskers to her tail. Gray . . . GRAY!

The powerful notion of what caused the change in her fur hit my brain, and in horror I watched her approach.

I stumbled off the deck and out to the edge of the woods, looking down to see . . . yes, indeed. Maggie had rolled in her dad's ashes. There was a perfect mold where she had pressed her feline body into the pile of ash. As I turned around, I could see her sitting on the deck, and even at this distance, hear her purrs.

To scream or laugh. Laugh or scream. Those seemed like my only two options. It took just a moment to decide. My laughter rang through the neighborhood. In truth, there had never been an option.

That story spread like wildfire, and in the process, Maggie became a legend.

CHAPTER NINE

I had hoped my halcyon days were here to stay. One can always hope.

A few days later, I was woken up at four A.M. to the sound of whistling. I lay in bed and willed myself to stay perfectly still. That was my plan to cause the whistling to stop!

As the whistling got louder, I became aware of other noises that seemed to increase in volume as well: the ticking of the grandfather clock . . . the sound of the refrigerator seemed to climb the veritable stairway and enter the bedroom as loud as thunder . . .

Then the music started. It was coming from the very walls of my bedroom, as if the room itself had turned into a huge CD player. Music and whistling engulfed me. My heart raced, and I broke into a cold sweat.

Maybe I was sleeping. Could you have an anxiety attack while you slept?

Just then, a new noise joined the others, one that truly terrified me more than any other.

It was the sound of a door opening. The creak of the bedroom door opening in an agonizingly slow manner.

The room filled with an eerie yellow light. There didn't seem to be a source. Just light, a light that seemed to move in waves. The door was opening further, from just a crack originally to wider and then wider still.

And then my husband walked into our bedroom.

"Hello, Regina. It's nice to see you again."

It felt good to faint.

I don't know what woke me up. It was probably about an hour later, and the new spring morning was coming up. The sun was just starting out on its always-new journey, and the birds were stirring faintly in their nests.

I lay in bed as I went over what had happened in my dream. I heard the whistling, and I heard music. I for sure saw Elliott, not Elliott as alive but a spirit kind of Elliott. His skin had almost a shine to it, and his face was tanned but without wrinkles. Even his hair shone. His hair! He was almost bald from the chemo when he died. But now this Elliott had hair. A fine gray hair cropped short like he usually wore it.

And then I remembered something else about the dream— how he was dressed! Not with his usual khakis (*never* jeans), and polo shirt . . . Elliott was dressed in a tuxedo. And he wore dancing shoes!

How the hell did I know they were dancing shoes, you might ask? We had never danced together in thirty years. Not even on our wedding day. It was something we just accepted like valets who took your car for a long joyride and older clients whose minds could turn in a variety of unforeseen directions. Elliott could not dance.

Now, he had tried to learn for years—I have to give him credit there. He'd taken all kinds of classes that promised him they would teach him to dance. They could not. He was even expelled from Arthur Murray School of Dance. Well, expelled may be a strong word, but his inability to learn became a kind of black eye on the particular instructor's flawless track record, so they convinced him to quit by giving him a full refund.

Elliott could not dance. So why was he wearing a tux with dancing shoes? Somewhere in my head, I had conjured up a dancing Elliott, and that thought made me laugh out loud. All I could do was mutter, "Lordy, Lordy . . ."

As I headed toward the shower, I was still laughing, feeling a good mood suffuse the beginning to my day. "Lordy, Lordy . . ."

I passed his dressing room, and with one glance in, I immediately stopped laughing. There in the middle of his dressing room, smack in the middle, right in the middle, sat a pair of dancing shoes.

The exact pair that had been on my late husband's feet not so long ago.

"Lordy, Lordy!"

I could not get out of the house any faster. I didn't shower, just grabbed at my clothes: anything, anything for shoes. I remembered to feed the cat, although later in the day I would discover I'd given her my can of tuna and threw the can of Fancy Feast into my lunchbag.

I jumped into my Mercedes and floored it out of the garage, never even stopping to admire my Cadillac of door openers. I made it to the office in record time, the windows down, the moon roof open, and the radio up high. I didn't stop to let the "guys" park the car, I just threw it against the curb and ran into the office.

I was early.

Carol looked up as I made my way into the office. I needed a safe haven, somewhere where nothing crazy was happening. At least not that kind of crazy. Expected crazy was fine.

"What's wrong with you?" Carol asked. "You look like you just saw a ghost."

"Bad choice of words. VERY BAD!"

"What happened?" Carol was now looking not only concerned but also a little scared. She brought me into her office.

Barely breathing I managed to stammer, "I saw a ghost. That's what it was. Elliott was in my bedroom this morning. Our bedroom. With a tuxedo and dancing shoes on."

Her reaction was not a laugh, not an F bomb.

"You believe me, don't you? Please tell me you believe me."

"I think I do," said Carol in almost the same strangled tone as mine. "Sit down. Try to relax. You want water, wine?"

Looking up at the suggestion of wine, Carol quickly added, "For you. Not for me. Although . . ."

"Do you believe me?"

"I do."

"Why?" I asked, not yet satisfied.

"Because I have never seen you look so upset in all the time I've known you. Plus, you have two different sandals on, and your jacket is misbuttoned."

One look down and yup, I was wearing one black kitten-heel sandal and one brown flip-flop.

"Carol, why are you holding my hand?"

"I don't know. I guess I feel I've got to do something constructive."

"Why? Why now? Why a tuxedo and velvet shoes? Everybody knows Elliott wouldn't be caught dead in shoes covered in fabric!"

"Well, actually he is dead, is he not?" Carol said with a grin.

That was my Carol. She gave me strength.

"Well, of course he is, but I saw him this morning. And there's more to it."

"What?" Carol's eyes closed partway as if to protect her against fully hearing whatever was coming next.

"After he disappeared, the shoes were still in his dressing room."

"Just sitting there."

"YUP."

"Let me ask you this . . . Could he have bought them for himself? Sort of an, I know I can't ski so I'll buy myself a ticket to Aspen and then I'll have to learn to ski?"

That brought on a span of silence as I thought about the logic of her statement.

"No. Elliott would never have bought dancing shoes to simply inspire him. He wasn't an aspirational shopper."

The silence continued as we both remained lost in our own worlds. Worlds that had seemed orderly just a few weeks ago. Measured by the same ruler everyone else was using.

Looking up at Carol, I reached up and grabbed her hand as she had taken mine earlier. This time it felt good. It felt right. She was my friend.

I knew she felt the same, and together we struggled to regain a semblance of what we could call normal.

"What are you going to do?"

"Well, I'm here . . . so I guess I'll work."

"I'm here if you need to talk."

"And the wine?"

"I didn't actually have any." She called out after me, as I left her office: "But I'll get some!"

Heading down the hall, I passed my secretary's desk to pick up messages. I noticed her staring at my unusual attire.

"Care to talk?" she queried.

"About what?" I asked, with just a trace of sarcasm. "Just making a new fashion statement."

"Does it have a name?" she retorted with an equal amount of sarcasm.

"Yeah. Chaos before dawn."

"Very catchy!"

CHAPTER TEN

I made up my mind to get some work done. Maybe that way I could distance myself from everything I'd been dreaming about, obsessing over, and even . . . witnessing.

I sat at my desk and willed myself to answer some calls. I wrote up some case histories, sent some emails—all things that normal people working normal jobs engage in. One would have to be in my position to appreciate the joy of such drudgery, the sheer relief it brought me!

Occasionally the mind-numbing spell of desk work wore off, and I stared into the distance. Each time I did, I had another vision of Elliott as he walked into the bedroom with that smile on his face. He seemed . . . what was the word for it . . . happy.

I was terrorizing the piles of paperwork on my desk, moving them smartly from the inbox to the outbox. Perhaps I should be tortured by hallucinations more often? Carol would like it—heck the whole state would benefit!

On the way home, I decided to drive by Mrs. S.'s. Even if she didn't come out of her home, her veranda beckoned to me as a place that was becoming more relaxing than my own back patio.

I pulled onto her street and walked up the path. When I started for the stairs, I heard her say in that inimitable voice, "You're a little late today."

The tone was part scolding, part positive coaching, like one might receive from a good parent. The statement surprised me, but not nearly as much as the formal tea she had set up on the table.

Such delicate cups and saucers. Blue and white with gold edges. Very elegant and, actually, very Mrs. Staples.

"You made tea," I said. I suddenly felt rather dumb. Of course she made tea.

"I guess I did," Mrs. S. said. "And it's a good thing, too—you are looking a little peaked today, Regina. Did you sleep well?"

Okay. Getting personal.

"No, actually. I didn't." Silence reigned, but not a totally uncomfortable silence.

"Is something ailing you?" Mrs. S. asked.

"Ailing me? Well . . . just a lot going on at work," I said, trying not to look at her. I was beginning to think this wasn't such a good idea after all.

More silence. "Would you like me to pour, dear?" Mrs. Staples asked.

I edged closer to her and watched her pour the tea into these perfect cups.

"Wedgewood?" I asked, indicating the maker of the tea service.

"Yes."

"Old."

"Very old, dear."

Mrs. S. poured as if she had formal tea every day. No shaking or spilling. Milk or not, one lump or two. Very professional.

We settled in. Mrs. Staples's dress was perfectly appropriate for afternoon tea, although it appeared to be linen rather than silk. A little early to wear linen, I thought. But who was I to talk, sitting there in my unmatched outfit, wearing two very different shoes? I wondered if she had noticed and decided she had not. I didn't think she could have passed on the opportunity to comment in her partly supportive, partly challenging way.

I wondered if Mrs. S. had ever run out of the house wearing two different shoes. I guessed not, judging from the way she drank her tea in such an elegant, ladylike manner—as opposed to me, who had to do all I could simply not to slurp. But then, Mrs. S. may not have had visions of her deceased husband to contend with while trying to get dressed this morning. . .

To my relief, she changed the subject:

"How is Pearl doing?"

"Pearl's great. She put Leo in a urinal last week."

"I beg your pardon! Did you say urinal?" She really blushed there. I wondered if she had ever said the word out loud before.

"Yeah, it's a Pearlism."

"A Pearlism?"

"I don't know why, but sometimes Pearl can really jumble up the English language," I said.

"How so?" At this point Mrs S. was listening with grave interest. I wondered if she saw herself in Pearl at all. Or wondered if a Pearl-like future awaited us all, her sooner than most because of her advancing age.

"When I first met Pearl she told me she had a 'hiatty herny.' It caused her a lot of pain. She couldn't eat or drink for days when it acted up. It took me a few weeks to decipher that a hiatty herny was a hiatal hernia. The funeral parlor was 'Gaggolly's,' when its actual name was Gallogly's.

"So when she called me the other day and told me she had put Leo's ashes in a 'urinal,' I just figured she meant an urn. Just a Pearlism. Just Pearl being Pearl . . ."

Mrs S. broke out in laughter, and I mean real laughter. It was the first time I had ever heard her laugh, and it was lovely and also infectious.

I found myself laughing, too. It felt great, so I traded a few more Pearlisms with her. And then I began to realize how comfortable I was with her. Just hanging out, drinking tea.

I started to share this with her, but she took the conversation in an unexpected direction.

"I am so glad you did not take this moment to express yourself as a social worker."

"What does that mean?" I asked, knowing exactly what she meant.

"Oh, you know. I am just so happy we could share a laugh together."

I didn't know what to say. I didn't know who was supposed to be helping whom. I needed more help than I was ready to admit, and that dimmed the comfort of the last hour a bit for me. But Mrs. S. didn't seem to notice. She sat there in her linen dress and sipped her tea.

"How are you doing with the dog walker?"

"Kid next door took the job. It's obviously not all-day jaunts in the neighborhood. But it's working. Oh, by the way, it's Bozo."

Mrs. S. regarded me. "Excuse me?"

"The dog's name is Bozo."

"Oh."

Once again, we sat there looking at each other while I wondered where we were going with all of this. Maybe somebody needed to come and sit on my veranda and check in with me? My suspicions were confirmed as I rose to leave.

"Just one more thing before you go, Regina. You are aware that you have on two different shoes and your jacket is on backward?"

"Yeah, I know. I'll fill you in the next time."

CHAPTER ELEVEN

The seasons in New England can be fickle. It could be sixty-five degrees on Thanksgiving and six below for Christmas. This season was particularly changeable; everyone was all abuzz, talking about "the year without a winter." For the most part we were loving it, even if it was part of the global warming process. To paraphrase my late husband: "Winter sucks."

Speaking of my late husband, things had returned to a relatively quiet place . . . no music, no whistling, and the velvet shoes remained in their same spot on the dressing room floor. I always felt very relieved when I did my daily check for dancing shoes: just a quick glance, and then I could move on for the rest of the day.

Feeling more sane than I had in weeks, I left the office one Thursday deciding to get something to eat before I drove home. I didn't have any food in the house, and even if I did, I never cooked. Cooking was something that Elliott took great pride in. Was I being true to his legacy by not ever turning on the new state-of-the-art oven I'd bought just after he died? For a moment I even felt bad for my virgin oven!

Barbara's Restaurant was relatively quiet in between the lunch gang and the crush of the dinner crowd. I sat at the counter and ordered a small tuna melt.

Not a lot of people knew that the chef had a crush on me and that he would make anything I wanted in a smaller version. I know of one other person who dared to order a smaller size sandwich, and he was sent away in a hurry. It was not pretty.

Charles (always Charles, never Charlie) sat down next to me, and we started to talk about the weather. The weather was actually a semi-interesting topic of conversation these days. While we were conversing, my attention moved over Charles. He was a big man, six foot three and two-hundred-plus pounds, but he had the smallest hands I'd ever seen on a man. Small and very feminine, not that I would ever tell him that to his face or anything.

Could I ever see myself dating this man, or any other man for that matter? Or would it be lifelong widowhood for poor Regina? Perhaps when I was further through the grief process, I would be better able to assess my progress in this direction. That process hadn't gone that smoothly at the beginning, but perhaps it was starting to pick up steam?

Charles was always dressed in white pants and a white shirt with a very red scarf tied at his neck. I don't know if it signified anything—Barbara's wasn't an Italian restaurant or anything—but I wasn't going to ask him that, either. Nothing that would invite any unwanted intimacy.

Instead, I leaned over and asked, almost in a whisper: "My valet guys, are they really former ACI inmates?"

"Yup."

"Does everyone know this except me?"

"Yup."

"Do I want to know where Slim takes my car?" Slim was the chief valet in charge of car sitting. He got his name because he was almost as tall as Charles but weighed nothing. When he stood sideways, he basically disappeared. Seriously!

"Probably not."

Carol had been right all along. She was right about a lot of things, I decided without any rancor on my drive home. Rather than compete with my friend, I decided to let it make me happy that I had a strong source of female wisdom in my life. Well, two, I suppose, if you counted Mrs. S. Could female friendships form an adequate substitute for the lack of a soulmate? Mrs. S. sure was doing okay. Better than me by a far stretch.

My Mercedes nosed out of the inner city, headed for the peace and tranquility of the suburbs. Even in the winter that wasn't, it was still nice to get home and cocoon a little bit. When I got home, I put on my favorite jeans, the ones with all the holes in them, and a comfortable, cotton T-shirt with an equally comfortable, cotton sweatshirt on top. This and a blanket and some TV were all I would need for the rest of the night.

I passed Elliott's dressing room and instinctively did a dancing-shoes check, the kind that had yielded a refreshing dose of no-news-is-good-news lately.

The dancing shoes were gone.

In their place sat my cat. In the middle of his closet was Maggie, purring and content.

As if expecting an answer, I asked her, "Where are the shoes? They're gone! What happened to them?"

"Well of course they're gone. They're on my feet."

I knew that voice. I mean I really knew that voice.

Ever so slowly, I turned toward it and saw Elliott standing in front of me wearing his tux and the velvet shoes.

"Hi, babe," said my late husband.

Vertigo came at me from the blue. I reached out and grabbed for the door.

"How is this happening?" I managed to whisper.

"Funny, coming from you. I thought you had this spirit thing all locked up!" Elliott started to walk toward me, and I hugged the door because I had nowhere else to go.

"Elliott. How did you get here?" I stammered.

"Well, we move pretty fast. It takes a little time and practice to master it, though. Right after I died, I tried to see you a couple of times . . . but I would slide right by you and sometimes wind up in embarrassing situations." Elliott laughed as he blushed.

"Spirits can be embarrassed?"

"Of course! But I'll wait a little longer to share some of my more miscalculated adventures with you."

I finally managed to croak out the question I wanted to ask above all of the other questions I could possibly ask. "What are you doing here?"

Elliott looked at me strangely. "I'm here to dance with you! Remember? We discussed this before I passed? I wanted to come back and waltz with you. I've even got the tuxedo and the dancing shoes. Pretty cool, huh?"

"Dance . . . Elliott, you don't dance." If he was going to use our pet name, then I would, too. "Babe," I said softly. "You never knew how to dance."

"Oh, I guess I forgot to tell you. I've learned to dance on the other side."

"Heaven! Are you talking about heaven! For Pete's sake! You don't believe in heaven!"

"Ssshhh. Babe, stop shouting. I don't mean heaven in the conventional sense, where everyone sits around on clouds and vegetates. The other side is a plane, it's, for lack of a better description, a state, where you wait until you move on to another plane."

"What the hell does that mean?"

"That's a different place," he said mischievously. "Let me begin again. A couple of times when I was in the hospital I died."

"How did you know? Did you have one of those out-of-body things?"

"Out-of-body experiences? I don't know what they call it. All I know is suddenly the pain stopped and I felt at peace. And you know what else . . . I could hear! My hearing was perfect."

Knowing how significantly hard of hearing he'd been, I was impressed. "Wow. What did you hear? Harps and things?"

"Of course not. Regina, I really thought you would be more familiar with this than you seem to be."

"Well, it might have to do with my state of mind. Did you ever think of that? That I might be in shock?"

Nice, Regina, I thought. *Your husband has returned from the afterlife or whatever, and you're taking the opportunity to quarrel with him.*

But he was unfazed. "Let me get back to my explanation of the other side. It was there that I felt the quiet. I was no longer restless. And I could hear!

"Regina, I could hear you cry. I heard you tell me to move on, but I wasn't ready, so I came back."

We looked at each other for a few very long minutes. Suddenly, he reached out to hold my hand; my skin tingled, but I felt a sense of warmth swell up inside my chest. I continued to hug the door until he dropped his hand.

Just then, the impact of what was really happening hit, and I began to cry.

"How is this happening?" I wailed into the dark. "How can I be talking to my dead husband?"

"Well, you are."

Once again, Elliott drew closer, and I was ready when he put out his hand. I grasped it, but then had to let it go just as quickly. I don't know what I had imagined, a cold, dead hand? Lifeless? It was none of those things; it was warm and smooth and wonderful. I reached for it myself, and as we sat across the dressing room hand-in-hand, I began to wonder about the meaning of all of this. The reason for all of this. And then I decided to just let it all happen.

At that point, Elliott started to fade—not that he changed color, but he began to sort of shimmer.

"Oh, dear, I've got to go. I thought I had more time. I'll try to stay a little bit longer next time . . . Oh, by the way? Please keep Maggie out of my dressing room."

"Why?" I asked.

"She lays on top of the dancing shoes and won't let me use them."

"What!" And he was gone.

I don't know how long I sat on the dressing room floor. I don't remember going back to bed or if I slept or cried. The next thing I knew, my alarm was going off, and a new day was about to begin.

All through breakfast, I wondered, *Should I tell anyone?* That seemed like such a crucial question before, but now it felt lighter, like everything wasn't so life or death. Which was a bad choice of words to describe that feeling, but there you have it.

As I dressed for the day and made my move out of my bedroom, I glanced into his closet, and the shoes were back. I can't honestly say I wasn't surprised . . . but I wasn't shocked, at least. I had my wits about me this time. Thinking of what he said about Maggie, I reached in and simply closed the dressing room door.

CHAPTER TWELVE

The next days sped by. I told no one of my encounter with Elliott, choosing instead to keep the whole episode wrapped around my heart. I knew I could never let it near my brain at this point.

Everything seemed lighter, I couldn't explain it. Like there was less to worry about. Situations came and went. They all seemed to just sort of resolve themselves.

One day, as I was getting ready to leave the office, the phone rang. I was anxious to test out my new equanimity, so I picked it up on the second ring.

"Hi, this is Regina."

"Hi, Regina. My name is Sharon, and I am a discharge planner from third floor north."

Perhaps my newfound balance would be tested, after all. "Third floor north" was another name for the geriatric psychiatric ward at one of the largest hospitals in the state. Rarely is a call from them good news.

"So, Sharon, what can I help you with?"

"Do you change locks?"

"I'm sorry?"

"Do you change locks?"

"What kinds of locks?"

"Apartment locks."

I was beginning to wonder if this was some kind of crank call, like a kid asking, "Do you have Prince Albert in a can?" ("Then you better let him out!")

"No, we do not do that kind of work."

"Oh! Do you know who does?"

"A locksmith, maybe. Just a guess but I think that is where you need to take this." *C'mon, Regina,* I thought. *No sarcasm. Back to equanimity . . .*

Sharon responded, "That won't work."

A moment of silence broke out. My curiosity reared its head. Fighting with that was the desire to just hang up and leave for the day.

Curiosity won.

"Sharon, what's the story here?"

It turned out that third floor north was currently hosting an eighty-eight-year-old lady who had committed a pretty serious suicide attempt. Her neighbor had her keys, and the patient wanted the locks changed before she went home.

"Why is she afraid of the neighbor? Why did she give him the key?"

"She decided to kill herself because she was all alone. Her family is all dead and she wanted to join them."

"Makes sense to me," I muttered, just out of Sharon's earshot. I mean, really, it kind of did.

"So, she told her neighbor of her plan. She was going to take a bunch of sleeping pills and die.

"It turned out that the neighbor decided to throw this woman a party. He invited the other neighbors, and at some point during the festivities, they began to suggest to this poor woman that she give them certain things in her apartment. After all, it wasn't like she was going to need them anytime soon. While dining over Chinese food, the neighbors began to take things from her apartment and bring the stuff to their own."

Unfortunately, you can't make stuff like this up. "Elder abuse" doesn't even seem to adequately cover the image of the La-Z-Boy recliner going down the hall to a new owner. Or various end tables and chairs stacked three deep in the elevator. Personal items like jewelry and linens were soon out the door as well, while copious quantities of beer and wine were consumed.

That night, per her plan, the client took her lethal concoction and prepared herself to meet St. Peter and her family. She laid down on her mattress, the bed's headboard having been taken by someone. The next thing she remembered was the sound of fists banging and someone calling her name. She opened her eyes, and, to her utmost surprise, she was not dead. She was in her bedroom, and as she lay there she realized that the pounding was actually in her head—she had a headache from hell!

The sound of someone calling her name was her neighbor standing over her, who, in a horrible whisper, said, "Oh my God. You are not dead."

"This is a joke, right?" I asked, with all the sincerity I could muster. But I knew what the answer was going to be.

"No."

And I was right.

"When did this happen?"

"Last Sunday."

"And you are just calling me now? Four days later!"

"Well, yes."

"When is she going home?"

"Tomorrow."

My equanimity was truly and fully gone by now.

Instead, I borrowed an expression from Carol. "Holy fuck!"

✳   ✳   ✳

The next day, I headed for the psych unit and met with the client, Mrs. Iverson. Yes, indeed, there had been a suicide send-off for her, and she had given all of her things away. But she was ready to go home now, and she wanted her things back.

I verified with the building manager that the locks had been changed. He wanted to know if I was going to take care of the bill for that. I told him to build it into her evil neighbor's rent the next time he was due for an increase. That conversation died soon thereafter.

Even though I didn't have a clue how I was going to do it, I promised the client we would figure out how to get her stuff back.

My next stop was the office where Slim waited for me to park my car. Feeling bold, I decided to ask him about his choice of parking venue.

"Slim, where exactly do you take my Mercedes when you park it?"

"Sometimes I take it to my parole officer's house."

"Why?"

"Because we sometimes meet there rather than his office."

"Why?"

"Well, sometimes there ain't any heat or lights on at the office, so he has our meetings at his house."

"Does the parole office know this?"

"Sure. They even encourage it," he said with a shrug.

Call me curious. "Why?"

"Then they don't have to worry about the heat or lights."

"Let me ask you this, Slim. Has your parole officer seen my car?"

"Lots of times."

"Well, isn't he curious as to how you are able to drive a brand-new Mercedes?"

"Nope." Again with the shrug.

"Hey, Slim, I've got to ask. What did you do, you know, to go south for?"

A small smile started at the corner of his lips, as I got the feeling that I really did not want to know the answer to my question.

"Boosting cars. I specialized in luxury models."

With that, the conversation was over. I left the city and went home. Sitting in traffic, I recounted my little talk with Slim.

A career criminal who steals cars drives my car to his parole meeting, held at the home of his parole officer—a sanctioned meeting, mind you—because the parole office does not have utilities. And no one thinks to ask the career criminal where he is getting a brand-new Mercedes.

At the next red light, I started to laugh at the absurdity. As it overwhelmed me, I put my head down and shook. Only a volley of car horns alerted me to the change of light, and I sped on. I was still laughing when I pulled in front of my home and dug out my sparkling-new garage-door opener. It was a beauty.

The laughing stopped when the garage door opened on its own.

CHAPTER THIRTEEN

Jesus, not again! I could literally feel the blood drain from my head down toward my feet. As the door slowly opened, the first thing I saw was a pair of velvet dancing shoes, and then I saw they were attached to my late husband's feet, which were connected to his legs and so forth—until the door had risen the rest of the way revealing all of Elliott in his tuxedo with his great, big, Elliott smile.

"Hi," he said.

"Hi," I said. "What are you doing here?"

"Waiting for you."

We faced each other, he standing inside the garage, me just on the outside.

"Were you responsible for the garage door going crazy?" I asked.

"Yes, I was," he stated. "And I am rather proud of it, if I might add."

The thought hit me, *What would the neighbors think if they came by to see me talking to myself in my garage? Or could they see Elliott?* I didn't honestly know how it worked, but I was beginning to suspect, ever so slightly, that this was not all the work of my imagination.

"Let's take this to the back deck," I suggested. "The people around here suspect I'm not too stable, and I don't want to give them any more ammunition."

"Probably a good idea."

As I made my way around the side of the house, I realized Elliott had disappeared. Where had he gone?

And up on the deck, to my utter amazement, there sat a glass of wine on the table with a candle placed delicately next to it.

"Took a lot out of me to open the wine, so could you light the candle?" Elliott seemed to materialize out of nowhere!

"Oh, sure," I said with all the newfound confidence that I was actually talking with spirits.

We sat there for a few minutes looking over the gardens. The young, spring flora was just beginning to pop, tiny buds were unfurling with the inexorable surge of life, and the smell that was making its way through the grass toward us was just incredible.

"Elliott, can we start at the beginning? Why are you here, and how did you get here?"

"Okay. Well, first, when I finally died, I went to a large garden—"

"Like the Garden of Eden?" I asked.

Elliott looked on in silence. "What's Eden look like?"

"Never mind. Go on."

"I sat there for awhile, and a young fellow greeted me; he told me he was to be my guide. He would share with me the rules of this new world and walk me through, explain my choices."

"What choices?" I queried him. "What possible choices do dead people have?"

"Regina, honey, calm down. Okay? Concentrate on what I am about to tell you. It's not every living soul who will be given the chance to hear what happens when a spirit passes over."

Regarding this point, I had to agree.

"When a death occurs, the spirit can stay with their body for some time, but at some point they must leave. Some souls go into the distance and are never heard from again."

"Is that like going to hell? Am I allowed to ask questions at least?"

"That word was never used. No one ever mentioned 'hell' or, for that matter, 'heaven.' Those souls just disappeared into the mist.

"My guide was very patient with me. He spoke in a quiet but very powerful voice. He told me I could leave the garden immediately and rest on a plane which resembled the garden where I was resting. There, I could gather my strength, and when I was ready, come back to the earth and be reborn."

"Reborn? Reborn to what? As what?"

"This particular situation offers little choice. When it is decided you are ready, you will come back into a body, but you may be a man or a woman, your culture and ethnicity will be completely different, and hundreds, even thousands of years may have passed."

"Is that like the normal way of doing it?"

"I'm just not sure what would be called normal in this situation, Regina. Then I was told of another way. Regina, are you paying attention? I could choose to return to the earth immediately and finish any things that had been left undone before I died. I could come back into my own body and interact with the people I loved. But in doing so, I had to bring happiness and fulfillment to other lost, living souls."

"I'm sorry, Elliott," I said, all trace of sarcasm now gone from my voice. "I don't think I'm getting this."

"It is a beautiful concept. Think about it, Regina. I can spend time here with you, and we can do something we were never able to do when I was alive. All we have to do is find some other folks to help them find their happiness. And Reg—since you are a social worker—I thought you could be able to find someone who needs help, if anyone could!"

"Oh, sure," I muttered. "I've got a flock of folks in need of spiritual fulfillment."

Here, Elliott adopted a very pensive gaze. "But I was told in all seriousness that this option should be taken only with a lot of thought, since, if this is to be my choice, it would not be guaranteed that I would come back as a human. Maybe a domestic animal, maybe not!"

"So my guide left me alone, and I began to think about our life together. It was perfect for me. I loved you as I never loved before. I trusted you as I never trusted anyone else. And you never asked for anything . . . Your smile was the only thing I saw when you walked into the room, and your smile was always just for me."

As he spoke, his skin began to change again; it was now shining.

"Are you going away again?"

"I don't think so. I think my soul is reaching out to touch you."

Suddenly, something touched my hand: a light brush, but a brush nonetheless.

"Is that you? Did I feel you touch me?"

"Yes, I think so."

My reaction to this miracle was that I jumped up, knocking over my glass of wine and spilling it onto the candle, which was then extinguished.

"You touched me?" I asked once again.

"I didn't mean to scare you."

"Elliott, you're a ghost! How did you think I would feel?"

The glass righted itself on the table, refilled with wine, and the candle was again lit. I sat back in my chair.

"How did you do that?"

"I just erased the moment."

"Oh." Nothing else would come out. I sipped the wine but never tasted it. I reached out to touch the candle, but it wasn't warm.

"May I continue?" Elliott asked. He seemed satisfied with his silence and went on. "So I sat in the garden and thought: What was the one thing we missed out on during our years together?"

"Is that a question?"

He nodded.

"Not having children?"

"I always thought you didn't want kids."

"I really didn't."

"So then that wasn't it. What was it we didn't do that could be so important? I thought as hard as I could—remember, this wish could make the difference between me coming back as a puppy or an Elliott you would recognize!"

This thought brought him to laughter, that sound that was reminiscent of the good old days. The days he was still alive!

"When my guide came back, I simply told him I want to learn to dance. I want to dance with my wife. I want to waltz with her around a dance floor. Please teach me to dance. All I would like to do is dance with my wife."

CHAPTER FOURTEEN

I never noticed the time as we sat out on the deck. Daytime turned to early evening, but only when it grew dark did it really occur to me I had spent several hours with my dead husband.

"So, have you learned to dance?" I asked.

"I'm working on it. I think everyone was a little taken aback by my total lack of ability at first. . ."

Warming to the topic, Elliott began to describe his dancing adventures in the garden as I sat and listened.

"First, they paired me with a young French lady who taught the Dauphin to dance at the court of Louis XVI. But when I told her of the fate of that particular royal family, she got really upset. . .

"So my next partner was supposedly the dance instructor who gave Fred Astaire his first lesson ever. But she really wasn't that good, so I didn't believe her."

"Why not?"

"I mean, maybe she was. But I bet Astaire was born dancing, probably started in the womb, so all she did was teach him a few things he already knew. . .

"My third partner was the trick. She looked like Loretta Young and smelled of violets."

"Yeah. You were always fond of violets."

I tried to remember if Loretta Young had been married to Clark Gable, and then suddenly I didn't want to hear about Elliott's dancing lessons anymore. I struggled to understand why. Then it hit me: I was jealous! Yup, jealous. I've been down here, on this plane or whatever you call it, struggling to deal with my loss and my grief—and not doing that well with it, I might add—while he's up on some other plane dancing with dead people.

"Well, that's mature!" Elliott said.

"What did you just say? Are you able to get in my head and read my thoughts, too?"

"I'm very new to that one perk, and I understand it takes a while to get efficient with it. But that last thought was so far out there, I was able to read it quite easily!"

"So when do we get to the dance part? When are we going to get to dance?"

"Oh, not y-e-t-t-t," he said, somewhat dismissively.

"Why n-o-t-t-t?" I asked, trying to mimic his tone.

The silence that followed was thunderous. I recognized my anger from the countless spats we had over the years. I'd usually say something stupid. Then he would react in a somewhat superior manner. I would re-react with something even more stupid, and he would come back with something even more superior, and we were off to the races. This had to stop now.

"Elliott, I'm sorry, but I really feel as if . . ."

His look silenced me immediately. "Regina, trust me. You are not . . ."

"Crazy," we both said at the same time.

"The time will come, and it will come soon," Elliott said. "And you need to believe in me. Be ready to listen and learn. And then I'll be back to dance."

And once again, I was alone.

Returning to my office the next day, I resolved to have a good attitude at work. If I had to wait, I might as well enjoy the present. You know, try to help people, be a good person—apparently, you never knew what waited for you after your life was over, and that might just include some judgment on your actions. In any event, it was becoming progressively clearer that death was not the end.

I treated each of my voicemail messages as special tasks that had been sent for me to fulfill. And the truth was, I was doing pretty well with what had been given to me. The locks to Mrs. Iverson's apartment were changed, and most of her belongings had been located and returned. Albeit, the headboard was still missing. My hoarder's fate had been sealed. The family had called in the reality TV people and, in exchange for getting his face on camera for a few minutes, he had agreed to cooperate completely. I never understood this about people—yes, you are on camera, but then the whole world will know your troubles . . . Who knows? Maybe that is part of the healing. Just putting it out there in the world; it was the same with Pearl, who was getting on with her grieving by starting a memoir to tell the world of Leo and their shared love.

The last message was from Mrs. Staples.

"Where have you been? I waited for you yesterday, and you stood me up."

Stood her up! What, were we going steady?

I put my feet up on the desk, thinking, *Boy we have certainly changed our tune . . .*

I called Mrs. S. back and reassured her I would be there by three. I finished some paperwork, all those pesky reports that administration wanted, accountability to the bean counters, even paperwork seemed like it had its place today. Is that what they call a miracle?!

By two thirty, I was getting ready to leave, when Carol reappeared.

"Where you going?" she asked, as she took a bite from her cookie. Where were all these cookies coming from?

"To see Mrs. S., and I'm already late."

"My car is in for service. Can you give me a lift to the garage?"

"Yeah, but hurry up."

Bursting through the front door onto the street, I stopped in my tracks. My car was gone. Oh my God. "Where's my car?"

Carol noted the panic in my voice, and I noted the derision in hers. "Where did you leave it?"

"Well, actually, I didn't leave it anywhere . . . Slim took it."

"Holy fuck! How can you keep trusting that guy with your car?"

Just at that minute, my Mercedes sailed around the corner with Slim behind the wheel. He brought the vehicle to a stop right in front of me and got out, sweeping his arms toward the open front door in an elegant fashion.

"Where were you?" I yelled at him.

"Had a late appointment with my parole officer."

"How did you start the car?" I asked, waving my keys in his face.

Slim just grinned. "I don't need no keys to start your car." Then off he sauntered without a care in the world.

From the passenger seat, I heard Carol mutter, "I do not have a good feeling about this."

"Me neither! Remind me to have a heart-to-heart with that young man tomorrow."

"You may want to bring a gun."

"Oh, for God's sake, Carol. I don't own a gun."

"Want to borrow mine?"

After dropping Carol off, I glanced at my watch and knew I had already blown my three o'clock appointment. *Well, Mrs. S. will understand,* I rationalized as I prayed to the traffic gods to be kind to me.

They weren't, and she did not.

I raced up to her veranda and stopped about halfway. Mrs. Staples sat in her usual chair, and her glare prevented me from effectively progressing.

"In my world, it is customary to call if you are going to be late."

"I am so sorry, but wait 'til I tell you what happened to me today. . . . You will understand."

"When did we have this role reversal?" Mrs. S. asked.

Role reversal? I thought. *What role reversal?*

She continued, point blank: "Let me clarify something. I am the client. And you are the professional."

"Yeah . . . but . . ."

"So it is customary for me to talk, and you to listen."

"I agree. Quite right. But . . ."

"Well, today, I have a few things to say."

The irony! The day had finally come for Mrs. S. to open up, and all I wanted to do was confess to her about my life and struggles.

"All right," I managed to say.

"And if we have some time at the end, you can share with me the story of your day."

CHAPTER FIFTEEN

Mrs. Staples sat as if bolted into her chair. Her hands were clasped, and it was as if I could see her brain turning in her head. She had something to say, but I had no idea what.

When she did speak, it didn't clarify matters much.

"What do you know about St. Brigit?"

"Probably nothing."

"I'm surprised. I would have thought a nice, Irish girl like you would be aware of her story."

"Wasn't around my Irish side much. As a matter of fact, I wasn't around them at all. But the name's familiar . . . St. Brigit. Was she a saint?"

Mrs. S. was not amused. "Of course. But before she was a saint, she was a goddess, and many believe she was a daughter of a druid."

"Sounds complicated."

"Do you know what a druid is, Regina?"

"Sort of like a wise man in ancient Celtic times?"

"A rather simplistic explanation, but yes, a druid was a person found in ancient times. But more than just wise. The member of a priestly clan. They possessed knowledge that went back to a time when the earth was new."

"Okay . . ."

"You know, Regina, you should read up on ancient Celtic history. You may need it someday."

I'm sure I would, I thought. *After all, my life had careened off the rails. Ghostly visitations, possessed electronic equipment . . . now I'm on a stranger's veranda being scolded as if she were my mother while she educates me about Irish mythology. Do some reading about druids? Why not?*

"Brigit was the patroness of the healing arts, of fertility, of poetry and music and agriculture."

"Wow, she is covering a lot of territory there."

Mrs. S. ignored me and continued, "She is associated with the changing phases of the moon, as well as the ox, the boar, and the ram. Her sacred number is nineteen."

She paused and glanced over at me. As she folded the material of her dress into pleats, she asked, "Does any of this sound familiar?"

"Nope."

Brigit patron of healing arts

"The people of Ireland believe she invented whistling and, perhaps, keening."

The silence weighed a ton. At that moment, the hair on the back of my neck stood up.

"Now I see I am getting somewhere with you," Mrs. Staples said in a very gentle voice I'd not heard before. "Keening is the mournful song of bereaved Irishwomen."

"I know what keening is."

She looked at me and again spoke very gently, "I know you do."

I was feeling a bunch of stuff flowing from my brain to my toes. She was starting something, something I just knew I couldn't control. I felt the need to get ahead of her and take over this conversation. Thinking quickly, I asked: "But why would anyone need to invent whistling?"

"It was a way of communication with the other priestesses in her group."

"Oh." I hated that answer, really hated it, but didn't know why.

"Regina, I know whistling and the whistler have been very important to you."

I was practically speechless. "How do you know that?"

"I know a lot more about you than you can ever imagine."

"Like what?" I asked, not really wanting to hear the answer.

"Your birthday is on the nineteenth day of the third month in 1949. And dear, you have the sign of the ox."

"So? You Googled me." I shrugged and added a sarcastic smirk for good measure.

"No, I did not. I'm not even sure what that is."

"I also know that your oldest sister was in the convent for several years and was named St. Brigita, or Brigit in other words, and that that was your father's favorite name."

This conversation was nothing I had bargained for or expected in my wildest dreams. My heart was racing, and for a few seconds I thought I might just faint. I'd forgotten all about my sister and the convent.

I could barely croak out the next few words. "What does this all mean?"

"Regina, I don't think your being led to my door was a coincidence, nor do I think your tenacity was personal. I think you were sent to me as an angel might be. I think we have an awful lot in common, and I think we are meant to go on a journey together. But it will all happen in good time."

The tension suddenly eased, and I gained some semblance of peace of mind until Mrs. S. said, "And now, Regina, it's time for you to share."

* * *

I was very still as I debated how much to tell Mrs. Staples. Back and forth went the pros and cons. Should I be the consummate professional and say nothing? Should I tell her a little? Tell her a lot? My brain was in overdrive.

I opened my mouth and didn't stop talking until my whole story was out. The whistling, the shimmering, the wine I couldn't taste and the candle I couldn't burn myself on, Christo, even those dreadful dancing shoes.

When I finally finished, I looked over, squinting to see if she believed me. I think the squinting was to soften the blow in case she thought I was a nutjob.

She seemed to be asleep. For the first time ever that I had seen, Mrs. Staples appeared to relax. Her hands were still in her lap, but her fingers were no longer wrapped in one of her death grips. Her breathing was peaceful, and her color had returned to a healthy glow.

But, of course, she was not sleeping. And I immediately felt we were at a place that truly represented the calm before the storm.

When Mrs. S. finally opened her eyes, they were filled with tears. When her sobs started, I feared they would never end. *My Lord. What have I done!*

Mrs. Staples held her head in her hands now, and I really had to stop myself from reaching out to comfort her. Slowly, very slowly, the sobs ebbed into soft cries, then they ended as well. We sat quietly in our own worlds.

And then she smiled, not her familiar, sardonic smile, but a smile that could best be described as radiant.

"Mrs. Staples, I am so sorry," I began. "Did I say something to make you sad? I don't recall having made a client cry like that before."

"Oh, my dear! I am not sad. Not sad at all."

"I know what I just told you may seem strange, okay, stranger than strange, weird to the point of being unearthly, but please tell me you believe me?"

And it was important that she believed me. I didn't really understand why it was so damn important for her to believe me. But it was.

Mrs. S. continued to look at me and simply stated, "Oh, I believe you. My dear, you have no idea how long I've waited to meet you and hear your story.

"Regina, I strongly feel that we are about to embark on a journey. You and me and Elliott. Yes, Elliott, too . . ."

"Where are we going?" I stammered, only to feel terribly embarrassed at my own naïvete.

For some reason, this made her laugh. "Oh, Regina, you do make me laugh sometimes."

"I do." I was astonished. "I can see that."

"I'm not sure where we are going. We may never leave this house, but we are going to travel, and when we come to the end our lives will be different, and hopefully our souls will be at peace.

"And we will have company. Other lost souls that will join us as we change our world. And, Regina, trust me on this—Brigit will be our guide."

CHAPTER SIXTEEN

Driving home was a challenge. Every bone in my body ached, and I was hot, so hot. I don't think I moved once while on the veranda except for the occasional breathing.

At home, I shut off the alarms and started to feed the cat, relieved to be in my own space until I noticed my husband sitting at the kitchen table with those awful slippers propped up on my wall. My very expensive silk wallpaper.

"Hey! Get your feet off the wall," I said, making an attempt to bat them down. All attempts were futile as my hands just passed through his feet.

"Well, hello to you, too!" Elliott said.

It was then I realized the complete craziness of this entire scene. It's funny the way humans adjust. One minute, I'm a hardheaded, practical woman, and the next I'm swiping at my deceased husband's feet and having long conversations with him . . . and he is giving me great advice!

Over the next hour, I told Elliott all about my meeting with Mrs. S. He listened to me as intently, as he always did when he was alive.

"Did you ask her how she knew all of this?" he asked.

"I did. But I don't think she was ready to open up. I think she wants to keep me in the dark a bit longer, although I'm not sure why."

"Did you tell her about me?"

"I did."

"And what was her reaction?"

"Strangely calm. After her crying spell, I mean. Then she was so calm it was almost eerie."

"So . . ." Elliott started in that tone of voice that always meant he was talking to himself as much as anyone. "Just who is this goddess Brigit?"

"I don't really know. Don't you have like a direct pipeline into information like that now? You know, a source that can fill us in?"

Looking at me with fondness, Elliott admitted he might have an "in" with his new connections. "Great idea! Well, got to go."

"Where are you going?"

"I'm going to do what you asked for, find out more about Mrs. Staples and her goddess B—"

"Can't you stay for dinner?" I interrupted.

For the first time since our conversation started—really since I'd started seeing him again after his passing—Elliott looked at me with very sad eyes. "I don't really eat anymore."

Feeling embarrassed, I just said quietly: "What a dumb bunny I am. Of course you don't. You're dead."

"See you," he said as he headed out the kitchen door. A thought entered my head: Why is he using the door?

The same thought must have entered his mind simultaneously because he turned to me laughing. "I keep forgetting I can pass through walls!"

At first, his light began to fade, but then, abruptly, Elliott began to shine. I felt a mixture of warmth and glee everywhere in my body, and I knew he was touching my heart.

"Elliott, I will always love you. There will never be another—emphasis on never!"

"Babe, that's a whole other topic for discussion!"

Days flew by until the first days of summer were upon us. Elliott had visited several times and been able to confirm what Mrs. Staples told me about the goddess St. Brigit. She was apparently a very powerful lady back in the day and still commanded a great deal of respect and adoration in Ireland.

After a gap of a few weeks, I visited with Mrs. Staples again. She was strangely quiet as she sat on her veranda. I wondered if she was ashamed of what she shared with me. Or if she wanted to take it back. Sometimes when people were quiet, it unnerved me, and then I tried harder to get a reaction from them in order to get them to talk. In Mrs. S.'s case, I chose to do this by bringing up the subject of her daughter.

"You haven't spoken to Paula in a long time," I said.

"I don't remember bringing up my daughter's name in any of our discussions."

Uh-oh . . . As one might notice, I always have something to say. Change that to often.

"Obviously, she was the person who initiated the referral," Mrs. Staples said, looking to me for affirmation.

Silence, without any affirmation on my part.

"No, if you must ask, or, rather, as you have stated: I have not spoken with Paula in a long time. I miss her very much."

"Can't you just call her?" I asked naïvely.

"No. That would be impossible."

"Why not?" I asked, keeping up the dumb routine, which was, for the most part, accurate anyway.

Something of a wind caught my sails, and I began: "The last time we spoke, you told me you believed my coming here was not a coincidence, but that the four of us were tied together on a journey. Well, three of us are in the schoolyard, and Paula is the only one outside. Maybe you need to bring her in."

"I can't."

Suddenly, I was angry with her. Her stubbornness. Her impossibility. What could be so goddamn important that it stood between me and my dancing with Elliott!

"I will not call her," she said in her clipped speech that I knew from a few months ago. The speech pattern that signaled coldness and solitude.

Frustrated, angry, and desperate, I decided it was best if I just left.

"Look. I've got to go. I'll see you next week."

This was met with a similar silence. As I turned to leave, I looked at Mrs. S. She seemed to have aged in the last hour. Her face was ashen, and the skin on her hands seemed loose. Even her normally crisp dress seemed to hang on her frame.

"Regina, I'm sorry. I will not call her."

"I get it," I said, waving my hands. "I get it, already."

And then, to my amazement, Mrs. Staples said, "Regina, I never said you couldn't call her."

Oh!

* * *

Over a glass of wine later that evening, Elliott asked me, "Are you going to call her?"

Well, I was drinking, he was not.

"Yes. Elliott, why are we being brought into this? Can't we just dance without Mrs. Staples and her daughter?"

"I don't know . . . For some reason, the four of us are attached on some other plane. We have some unfinished business with each other. I'll check into it, but I doubt it. I'm pretty sure I will be told something like, 'It is written.'"

"Christ!"

"Did I tell you I met him?"

"Who?"

"Christ. Nice, young man, very modest."

"Jesus Christ is modest!"

"Oh, yes. He really does not get what all the hoopla is about . . ."

The absurdity of the situation hit me again. Sitting on my deck with my dead husband, talking about Christ, whom he had apparently met. The words tumbled out:

"I miss your laugh. I miss your smell. I miss our life. Sometimes I think I can't go on . . . I'm stuck."

Elliott became very intense. "Stop it, and stop it now. You knew what you were signing up for years ago by marrying a man fifteen years older than you. When all this starts to make sense and Mrs. Staples gets what she wants, and we get to dance, I'll have to leave. That was my bargain with the Masters. You need to move on. Get a boyfriend, go out . . . Write a book!"

"A boyfriend? I have no interest . . . and write a book *on what*?"

"On us and our extraordinary love. Let people know that blessed love is possible. Tell them the story that should never have happened.

"For God's sake, Regina, give them hope."

CHAPTER SEVENTEEN

The next day, I called a staff meeting. I was determined to leave behind the land of hazy spirits and stubborn old ladies and give my full attention to my job and my clients, if they would have me.

My kids came into my office looking very skeptical and shy.

"Wazzup . . ." said my case aide in his best effort to fit into our neighborhood.

"Knock it off," I said. "Your Brown degree is showing."

With everyone sitting around the table, I asked for case updates. This was greeted by silence.

"What, no problems to talk about?"

Again, silence.

"Everybody's getting along famously? No square pegs struggling to be put in round holes? No unconscionable delays in paperwork processing from other departments? C'mon, seriously?"

The nurse case manager, and apparently the group's unofficial spokesperson, said, "You haven't asked any of us for a review in weeks. Why now?"

"Well, I've been a little preoccupied for the last couple of weeks."

"More like months," said my newest case aide, a young lady who was usually quite shy.

"Where did *that* come from?"

"I don't know."

I looked around the room trying to get a grip on a growing fear in my belly. Here were three people who were very important to me. Not just as staff, but as friends, too. Tom and I had been together from the beginning—we shared more than twenty years of bumps and bruises. Betty, the RN, had come on board as a hospital staff nurse and took to the crazies out there like a duck to water. And my newest gem, Alicia, had come in as an isolated young lady with a wimpy handshake and was discovering her life with increasing gusto.

"I guess I should tell you that we are pretty angry with you," Tom said as he bounced uncomfortably in his chair.

"Why?"

"Because you haven't been here lately."

"I've been here! I haven't been sick a day!"

"Maybe I should qualify that," Tom said, rather smugly. "Your body has been here. But your head has not."

I suddenly realized I could not remember the last time any of them had been in my office. Or the last time anyone had even asked me a question.

"Well, who has been doing the hands-on daily supervision, then?"

"Carol," Tom said. "And—"

"And?"

My youngest spoke up with confidence. "And Dr. Piffs."

So glad she was growing into her own at my expense. "Piffs, are you kidding me! How the hell desperate have you been?"

"Very desperate," Alicia said.

"Morbidly desperate," Betty said.

"Idiotically desperate," Tom said.

I felt such sadness as I looked at this trio of good people.

"I am so sorry," I began, "but my life is complicated now."

"Your life has always been complicated," Tom said. "But you always included us on the merry-go-round."

My thoughts were jumbled. Should I let them in on what was going on? Would that reflect badly on myself as their supervisor? Perhaps I had strayed so far from the path of being a good leader that this was the only way to earn back their trust? But how could my story do that?!

Talking with my dead husband and planning to dance with him because he learned how to dance in the afterlife would make them question my sanity.

"Okay," I said. "Are you sure you want to be a part of my world?"

All three nodded yes.

I closed the door and was tempted to lock it. After all, that would give me a chance to subdue one of them should they choose to go screaming into the proverbial night with my news. But I didn't.

"So here we go. You all know how difficult it has been for me since Elliott died. Well, it's not just that.

"He wants me to go dancing with him."

Tom was the first to speak. "That's it? That's been the reason for your tension and aloofness?"

"You don't think that's a good enough reason? Talking with my dead husband and planning to dance with him because he learned how to dance in some garden?"

"For you, no," Betty said. "I thought you had an ongoing relationship with his spirit ever since he died. Although the idea of you two dancing is kinda unique."

I looked at my merry band of case managers and marveled at their loyalty. I questioned their sanity, as I did my own—but I loved the loyalty!

As I sat with this group, I realized that for the first time in a very long time I was feeling relaxed. Like I could stop running for a second. Like we could talk about anything that might happen to come up . . . Then a thought popped into my head that knifed the relaxation balloon and sent shivers down my spine.

"What's wrong?" Tom asked.

"Oh my God!" I cried. "Elliott has spent all this time learning to dance—yearning to dance with me—taking really big risks to dance with me—and I just realized something. It had been so long since I even entertained the notion of dancing . . . that I don't think I know how to dance!"

"Problem. *Big* problem," Alicia stated.

"Holy cow!" This from the nurse.

"Now, this," Tom agreed, "this is a real nightmare."

∗　∗　∗

After my meltdown in the meeting, we brainstormed for an hour.

"Did you ever know how to dance?" Alicia asked.

"I don't know. Maybe as a kid? I mean I could do the twist and stuff like that . . ."

Annie looked at Tom and muttered, "'The twist.' That's a dance?"

Her dubious face made me laugh.

Betty jumped up and ran out of the office, sprinting back in with a cassette player, the kind normally used to tape notes. "Does anyone have music?"

"What kind of music do we need?" Tom asked.

"A waltz," I said.

That stopped the enthusiasm dead. All that could be heard now were groans.

"Can't you do something more modern?" Betty encouraged. "You know, more up to date."

"Such as?"

"Rihanna, Katy Perry, Britney Spears, even Madonna." This was Alicia's list, obviously.

"No, I'm sure he only learned to waltz."

"Wait a minute!" Tom interjected. "I've got an idea. Piffs has those inspirational tapes she plays in her office."

"And?"

"And some of them are bound to be in three-fourths time, which is the same as the measure used for waltzes. It's a staple of the New Age."

I looked at Tom like I had literally never met him before. "How the hell—"

Alicia interrupted me. "Let's get them! But how? Is she in?"

Tom hurled himself out the door. "I checked the parking lot. She's not in."

"Her office will be locked," stated my nurse. "She always keeps it locked."

"But I know where she keeps a spare key!" I practically yelled in triumph.

"Come with me . . . Not you, Tom," I said, as we ladies headed for, what else, the ladies' room.

We were causing a stir in the office. Heads popped out of cubicles and folks stared after our little parade. A couple women looked after us longingly; women always like to go to the bathroom together. A man would never understand.

The ladies' room was empty. "The key is in the second stall behind the toilet," I said.

We all ran for it, only coming to rest with all three of us inside the stall. I silently muttered a prayer that no innocent person would need to pee in the next three minutes, or else we would likely have to take any witnesses as prisoners.

"Give me some room! I can't get at it with everyone in here . . ." I squeezed behind the toilet and put my hand on the porcelain. My hand touched something cold. "Got it!"

"Eureka!" shouted Alicia.

"Huh?" Both the nurse and I looked over, shaking our heads.

"It was a question on *Jeopardy* last night. What did Archimedes say in the bathtub? 'Eureka!' It means, 'I got it!' He said it when he discovered something about finding the volume of irregularly shaped objects through the displacement of water . . ."

Who were these people? And to think I had been neglecting this fine collection of intellects!

"Eureka," I said, patting the top of her head. "I got it!"

Flying out of the john, we met up with Tom, then calmly proceeded to the vicinity of Piffs's office. Now was the tricky part; we had to all act like we belonged. Tom did the deed of opening the door, so he would be on the hook for breaking and entering, while the rest of us were just accomplices. Then we all strode in as if this were a planned meeting in her office, albeit without her there.

"Wow, she is neat," Tom said.

"A little OCD if you ask me," I muttered under my breath, yet loudly enough for all three of them to turn to me and stare.

Neat was the operative word. Her desk was bare except for a telephone. No yellow stickies, no files, no piles of legal pads. Everything was labeled. In Box. Out Box. Garbage Can. There was no label on the tissue box, and, of course, with my luck, no little sign telling me where the music was housed.

"Where are the tapes?" I practically shouted. Part of what was causing my angst was my feeling guilty for having diagnosed the good doctor. Or for my staff hearing me diagnose the good doctor . . .

"Right next to the tape player," called out the nurse, holding up several cassettes. "Where else?"

"Here, everyone grab something and see if there is any music we can use. Remember, we are looking for something slow."

In just under a minute, Betty let out a cry. "I think I found something!"

"What is it?"

"It's by Christo."

Uh-oh!

"I can't stand that dude's music," Alicia said.

Tom took the cassette out of Betty's hand, while I just stood there with my mouth agape. "No," he said, "this could work."

"What makes you think that?" I asked, feebly.

He held it out to me. "Look! She's got all the different songs designated as to what they can be used for."

"Of course she does."

Tom practically threw the tape at me. And sure enough on the case, written in Piffs's neat, neurotic handwriting, each track was labeled: DINNER FOR ONE – UPBEAT & INSPIRATIONAL; RAIN MUST FALL – INTENSE ALMOST ANGRY.

"Go to the next-to-the-last track," Tom said.

And there it was: THE WALTZ – NOSTALGIC CLASSIC WOULD MAKE A GREAT WALTZ.

"Eureka!" I yelled.

CHAPTER EIGHTEEN

Sitting on the front stoop later that evening, I thought about my quandary. I sat there because I was afraid that if I sat on the deck then Elliott would visit. I don't know why I thought that would make a difference—as a disembodied spirit, or whatever he was, I'm sure he could find me if he wanted to. Maybe he sensed that I needed my space and stayed away for that reason. I kept dreading he would show up, because I really did not know how to tell him I didn't know how to dance.

Tom had been correct; the music was perfect. Not only the waltz, but the rest of the tape as well; I couldn't find the track that had played in my bedroom during one of Elliott's early visitations, but it didn't matter because the energy in all of the music was the same. It suffused my office when I played it there, surrounding me with thoughts of Elliott and the very strange life mine had suddenly become. Begrudgingly, I even had to admit that if the tape had been found in Piffs's office, then she must be okay somewhere, as well. This glimpse of a softer stance toward Piffs was just another wondrous event of the last several months, but one issue remained: I still could not dance!

No amount of moving around the room with my three partners earlier had elicited anything remotely resembling a waltz from my body. The tune inspired me, and my soul was ready, but my feet remained firmly planted on the office carpet.

All the years of blaming Elliott for his inability to dance, and it had never occurred to me that I couldn't dance either. Suddenly, the whole situation became ludicrous. I started to laugh and laugh until I cried. I don't know what my neighbors thought of me as they walked by my house. "There she goes again, that crazy redhead sitting all by herself, with a glass of wine, laughing herself silly . . ."

And for the first time, I remember thinking, *Frankly, my dears, I don't give a damn.*

The next day as I headed toward the office, I found myself heading left at a Y intersection and following the road all the way until I ended up at Mrs. Staples's house. Somewhere in my morning commute I had subconsciously decided to stop and see if she had changed her mind about calling her daughter.

She most certainly did not. When I brought up the notion again, her body shot up into that ramrod-straight position and she turned her head away. No use going down this road again, at least not right now, so, as we sat on her veranda and sipped tea, I decided to fill her in on the latest developments in my life. She listened patiently. But with each passing second, I could feel the air grow thick with tension.

Then she stated, "You have to fix this. You simply have to dance with Elliott."

I was astounded by her force and stamina.

"You need to dance!" she repeated, practically spitting out the command.

"Yeah, yeah, I know this. But I don't see how it's going to happen. And why are you so upset, anyway? Isn't my delusion my own problem?"

"It isn't a delusion, Regina, and you know it. It is real, real for you, and real for me."

"Whoa! Wait a minute. I'm lost. When did you get so wrapped up in all of this?"

Mrs. Staples continued to drink her tea, but I could sense a change in our direction.

Suddenly she leaned toward me and asked, "Why don't you call my daughter?"

Yup, we were definitely sailing in new water now!

"Holy shit crap, where are we going with that?"

"Regina, you need to focus. You need to call my daughter, and then you need to learn how to dance. Those are the next two steps in the plan that is unfolding."

"Now there's a plan? Mrs. Staples, not for nothing, but I think you are oversimplifying this a little bit. Sure, Elliott learned how to dance, but do you know where he learned? *In heaven.* Now I don't know that much about what goes on up there, but I'm going to guess things come a little easier."

Mrs. S. stopped me mid-soliloquy and said, "Lessons are lessons. It doesn't matter where you take them."

I truly had nothing to say to such logic but sat there dumbfounded as I looked at her.

"What is your schedule for today?"

"I don't know. Why?"

"Can you be here for four o'clock?"

"Why?"

"Can you?"

I shrugged. "Yes."

"Please wear comfortable shoes, not the heels you have on now."

"Don't like my Uggs, huh?"

That got me a look.

"And Regina? When you get to your office, call my daughter."

"What do you want me to tell her?"

"Tell her I said it's time."

"*It's time.* That's it? *It's time.* It sounds so action movie. Can't I just whisper *The eagle has landed?*"

"You are to tell her, 'It's time,' because it is. And that's why I need you to be here at four P.M. this afternoon, sharp. I've told you before that we four are tied together, and now I will tell you that our time is very limited.

"The goddess Brigit will not wait for us, so we must be ready."

The goddess Brigit, my ass! I thought to myself.

She saw the look of incredulity on my face and said, "You don't believe all this now, Regina, but before the month is over, you will change your tune."

As she entered her home, she simply repeated, "You will change your tune."

CHAPTER NINETEEN

With Mrs. Staples's words ringing in my ears, I tossed around some of the scenarios that could happen at four o'clock that day. Obviously, it had something to do with dancing, but—no offense to Mrs. S.—she wasn't too spry at her age . . . how could she be so sure that she held the key to my lack of grace? Were we going to hold a séance with the goddess Brigit, and have her teach me how to dance?

Deep in reflection over these possibilities I pulled up next to Barbara's Restaurant, and Slim came out to take possession of my vehicle.

He looked at me with the saddest face and muttered: "You are so screwed."

"What? What are you talking about?"

"I'm telling you, baby girl, that the good times are over. That lady doctor wants your head."

"What lady . . . Piffs?"

"If that's her name."

"What did I do to her?"

"Something about taking a tape out of a locked office?"

"Oh, shit! *Oh, holy shit.*" I felt my whole body turn to stone.

Did I remember to put the tape back yesterday? That was the plan: steal—er, liberate it—listen to it, and replace it before anyone could notice it missing.

Before I disappeared into my building I stopped and looked back at Slim.

"How do you know all of this?"

"I got my connections. Keys, please?"

I tossed him the keys and headed for my office. Alicia came running at me like a Patriot linebacker and took me down a side hall.

"You are so screwed!"

"So I've been told."

"Piffs knows about the tape. She is in Carol's office, and she is really, really pissed."

"I thought we were all going to take the blame, remember? That's why we had four of us doing the breaking and entering, so we would all only get twenty-five percent of the blame? Where is the tape, by the way?"

"Sitting on Carol's desk."

"How did it get there?"

"Piffs found it on your desk this morning."

"SHIT. SHIT. Is that why we're not all going quarters on the blame anymore?"

Alicia nodded just as the door to Carol's office flew open. I knew by the way she looked at me that there wouldn't have been any way to share the blame in the first place. I was the senior person involved; I was the boss of all the other people on the burglary squad. All that was left was for me to not get anyone else in trouble besides myself.

I held my hand up. "I know. I am so screwed."

Carol didn't indulge in any amusement. "It's worse than that. She wants your head, but more important, she wants your job."

"That so?"

"Yes . . . What the hell were you thinking? Why steal a tape for chrissakes? Why not just go buy one yourself?"

"Steal is a pretty harsh word. I borrowed it, and I was going to give it back."

"You used her spare key to open a locked door, rifled through her personal belongings, and took something that was found in your possession more than twenty-four hours later. That makes a pretty strong case for using the word steal."

Piffs entered the hall. "I was wondering where you went," she said in her best pissed-off voice. "Consorting with the enemy, I see."

"Oh for God's sake, Piffs," I said, "let's not get melodramatic here. We can discuss this like professional adults."

Pointing directly at me but not speaking to me, Piffs said: "I would not put her in that category. I have a phone consultation in a few minutes, and after that I will return to discuss the proper course of action here."

As she left, I mimicked just loud enough for her to feel, if not hear, ". . . proper course of action here . . ."

Carol brought me into her office. "I know I am not going to like your reasons for taking the tapes."

"One tape. And I borrowed it."

Carol only muttered, "Fuck."

"Okay, why did you take the tape?" she began again in her best clinical voice.

"I *borrowed* it, because I really need to learn how to waltz, because it dawned on me yesterday that Elliott has learned to dance and I can't. So we decided to borrow a tape and maybe I could learn how to dance. We needed to find something resembling a waltz . . ."

"Who is we?"

"What?"

"You said, 'we.'"

"No, I didn't."

"Yes, you did."

"No, I didn't."

"Yes, you did. Twice. I do not like the word 'we.' Please tell me you are alone in this prank?"

So much for being the brave leader with the stiff upper lip.

Carol was literally pacing the room. "Your staff, too?" she yelled.

I nodded yes.

"I'm trying to help you here, but this keeps getting worse. Tell me, Regina: What's the rush? Why couldn't you wait for her to come back and ask to borrow her tape? Where's the frickin' fire?"

"Well, Mrs. Staples has finally given me permission to call her daughter and tell her 'it's time,' but even before that, I visited with Mrs. S. and she thinks we're on some kind of celestial timeline. The goddess Brigit has her special day, and that's when Mrs. Staples gets her daughter back and I dance with Elliott. Do you get it?"

"NO! No, Regina, I don't get it. No one could get that." Carol looked positively shocked. It was obviously an emotion she wasn't very familiar with.

"Mrs. Staples keeps intimating to me that it could happen at any time. Although I'm not exactly sure what 'it' is, but it doesn't matter—I still can't dance, and Mrs. S. won't get her daughter, and Elliott will have to return to his plane, and all the sacrifices he's made will be for naught."

"For 'naught'?" said Dr. Piffs. "Who says 'naught'?"

We both jumped. Neither of us had noticed Piffs had returned to the office.

Carol tried to take control of the situation. "How long have you been standing there?"

"Long enough to assess our little friend here and know she needs major medication," Piffs retorted with her hands secured on her hips in defiance.

"Look, I know you think I'm nuts, and maybe I am, but this is a real crisis."

For the first time today, Piffs seemed to lose some of her angry energy.

"I need to learn to waltz, and I need to learn to dance as soon as yesterday."

No more "we's," Regina, I coached myself.

"So *I* thought if *I* could listen to a waltz, I could at least learn enough to fake it. So I took the spare key and borrowed your tape."

"Did it work?" Piffs asked.

"No."

"So what are you going to do next?"

"I guess I'll have to tell Elliott that I can't dance."

"You were planning to dance with your dead husband?"

Carol remained quiet while I dug my hole deeper and deeper.

"Dead is such a final word. I prefer late . . . or even passed."

"And you have included Mrs. Staples, a client, in this delusion?"

"I'm beginning to think she included me first."

Dr. Piffs clearly didn't know what to do with this information. Sitting across from me, she merely shook her head.

"Listen," I said to both of them. "I have to go. I have to find comfortable shoes before I meet with Mrs. Staples this afternoon.

Then, turning to Piffs alone, I said, "I'm sorry. I am sorry I took the key and broke into your office; I am sorry I stole the tape. I violated your space, and if you want to get me fired I'll make it easy for everyone and just quit. I did what I think I needed to do, and to tell you the truth I would probably do it again, but I'm still sorry for causing you any shock or upset." I looked at Carol. "You guys can tell me later whether I still have a job, okay?"

Carol looked tired but calm, and I felt . . . almost nothing.

And then Dr. Piffs said, "I just wanted an apology, but I never thought I would get one from you. Never."

"So, is this over?" Carol asked.

I looked at Piffs, and she nodded. "Time to move on."

Out in the hall, Carol tugged at my sleeve. "One more question? How did you know where the spare key was?"

"Slim told me a couple of months ago."

"Holy shit," muttered Carol. "Maybe he does work here!"

CHAPTER TWENTY

As I prepared to leave the building, Mrs S.'s words rang in my ear, "Call my daughter."

I hunted for her file, but I could not find it. It was not in the usual place, i.e., the large messy-ish pile of files of my ongoing cases where I could still find things with lightning speed. It was not in the locked drawer full of files either.

What made me look under my desk I do not know! But there it rested. *Why would I put that file under my desk? Please, please, please, Elliott, don't tell me you are coming to bother me at work and playing your pranks here, too!*

I found the daughter's phone number; it looked like her work number, as it had an extension. But even then, I was not prepared when the operator answered:

"Episcopal Church of Boston."

That surprise would become an itty-bitty, baby surprise compared to the one I experienced when I asked to be connected to the extension and the operator said:

"I will see if the bishop is in. May I ask who is calling?"

Fortunately, my name appeared on the top of the Staples file, as it does with all of my cases; I mention that because at this moment seeing my name made it much easier to remember just exactly who I was.

A slightly recognizable voice answered. "Hello? Are you calling from Providence?"

"Yes," I said. "Are you Mrs. Staples's daughter?"

"Yes."

I reintroduced myself, and the bishop said, "Yes, I remember, you were highly optimistic about your ability to work with my mother. Told me there were no 'nuts you couldn't crack,' as I recall?"

Did I actually say that? Probably . . .

"How is that going?"

"Well, it's a little difficult to judge how well I am doing . . . since your mother seems to be calling all the shots."

"Some things never change. May I ask the reason why you are calling me now?"

My mind went blank for a minute, then I remembered to deliver my message: "Because 'It's time.'" When that didn't seem to be enough, I added, "The goddess Brigit?"

Silence, so I added one more time for good measure, "It's time."

A very loud and long silence.

"Are you there?"

"When will you be speaking with my mother again?"

"Well, actually, I have an appointment to see her today at four o'clock."

"Today?"

"Yes."

"Tell her I will try to work something out."

"What does that mean? Is that more code, like 'It's time'? 'Work something out'?"

"No, it's not code for anything. I have a very busy schedule this weekend. I'm a—"

"I know, you're a bishop. Weekends are crunch time. Well, this may just be a guess on my part, but I don't think 'I will try to work something out' is going to make her happy."

"Could you hang on for a moment?" The bishop put me on hold.

These Staples chicks were really pretty strange when you thought about it. Oh, and something worth noting: The Episcopal Church does not believe in hold music.

"Hello? Hello?" The bishop was back. Did I detect a little panic in her voice?

"Yes, I'm here."

"Tell my mother I will be at her home on Sunday at one P.M."

"Can I ask why you don't tell her . . . yourself?"

"I'd rather you tell her."

"All right."

Then the bishop said, "I will meet you there on Sunday."

"Oh, no! Not me. I don't work on the weekends."

"This Sunday is the beginning of summer, and this year it falls on the nineteenth . . ."

Okay, now I don't need my Farmer's Almanac.

"What do you and my mother discuss exactly?"

"Well, lots of things."

"You don't know about Brigit or the summer season or the number nineteen, do you?"

"Well, a little bit," I said defensively.

"I will see you on Sunday," the bishop said before she hung up the receiver. The apple in this case appeared to land at the foot of the tree.

And speaking of the tree, I would be late if I didn't get a move on. As I ran out to my car, I spotted one of Slim's cronies standing near my car.

"Where is he?"

"Who?"

"Slim."

"Don't know exactly."

Not feeling particularly comfortable with this character, I asked him to let Slim know I wanted to speak with him.

"Tell him yourself," he muttered and gestured to the corner.

Gazing over, I saw Slim pull into a parking spot driving a brand-new, very red BMW X5. Slim parked his new buggy and walked over to me and his fellow hoodlum, strutting all the way.

"Where did you get that?" I queried.

"Borrowed it."

"From whom?"

Slim shrugged. "Let's just say I liked your theory on borrowing versus stealing something."

"What are you talking about?" Pretending naïvete wasn't going to work, but at least it made me feel better.

"You know, your explanation to the good doctor about the tape you borrowed from her? She said you stole it, and you said that since you intended to give it back it wasn't stealing, it was borrowing."

"What the hell does this have to do with that Beemer?"

The smile on Slim's face could light up a stadium, but it was the twinkle in his eye that held the special demonic quality.

Reality hit. "You stole it!"

Slim responded, "I borrowed it with intentions of giving it back. I bow to the master."

"If, or should I say, when, you get caught, I hope that's not your only defense."

"Why not? It worked for you," Slim said as he entered the restaurant.

Shaking my head, I started for my own vehicle when I heard Slim's crony mutter: "That man is a genius."

CHAPTER TWENTY-ONE

Driving through the streets of Providence, I was besieged with thoughts: What if I didn't learn to dance? What if I *never* learned to dance? Would Elliott have to pay some kind of penalty for my ineptitude? Would the powers-that-be hold it against me? How would that impact the journey of Mother and Daughter Staples? Because I was in such a fog, I took a few wrong turns and ended up lost, which kind of reminded me of my life itself in this moment.

When I finally got back on the right road, the phone rang. It was Carol, beside herself with excitement about something. When I got her to slow down and speak English, she related the following conversation she had just had with the good doctor herself, Piffs.

Carol: "I really want to thank you for letting the whole thing with Regina go."

Piffs: "I'm surprised I let it go. I had no intention of letting it go."

Carol: "What changed your mind?"

Piffs: "Well, it turns out it was just Regina being Regina."

Carol: "You gotta love her!"

Piffs: "I wouldn't go that far, but she is beginning to grow on me. By the way, what's with the waltz and the dead husband?"

Carol: "It's a long story. A really long story."

Piffs: "Is she a sensitive?"

Carol: "You think Regina is sensitive! She's the most insensitive person I know."

Piffs: "Not sensitive. *A* sensitive."

Carol: "What's that?"

Piffs: "A person that sees spirits."

Carol: "Do you really want me to answer that? Well, I've known Regina a long time, and I will admit there is something odd about her."

Piffs: "Odd?"

Carol: "Maybe odd isn't the right word."

Piffs: "Spiritual."

Carol: "No! Definitely not spiritual. It's just that . . . sometimes she knows things . . . that she really shouldn't know."

Piffs: (Silence.)

Carol: "Like, after my husband left me several years ago, Regina asked me why he had a safe installed in his trunk of his car."

Piffs: "Did he?'

Carol: "I didn't think so. That sounded crazy!"

Piffs: "But?"

Carol: "But it turns out he had stolen a bunch of silver coins my dad had left me. I didn't know they were gone for years. Then one day, about two months after he died, Regina

125

told me where I could find the coins. I followed her lead and found out he had a safe installed in his trunk when he stole them because he planned on driving cross-country with them."

Piffs: "Did you ask her how she knew?"

Carol: "Of course! She told me, 'Don't ask.'"

Piffs: "Ah!"

Carol: "She seems to know . . . well, you know, she'll say, 'Gee, we haven't seen Elaine for months,' and within ten minutes, guess who walks through the door?"

Piffs: "Elaine?"

Carol: "Right. And, this may not be relevant, but I happen to know that our Asian clients, they think she is a 'white witch.'"

Piffs: "What's a 'white witch'?"

Carol: "Someone who walks in the world between life and death. And Spike, et al., thinks she is spooky, but they all really love her and respect her. And now that I'm thinking about it . . . how does a psychiatrist in your standing know about a *sensitive*?"

Piffs: "Are you ready for this?"

Carol: "I am."

Piffs: "I used to be one."

Carol: "Holy fuck!"

Dialogue-related, Carol came to a stop, as did I, easing my car into a parking spot along the side of a street I did not recognize.

Carol asked me, "What do you think of that?"

I said, "I'm lost again. That's what I think."

CHAPTER TWENTY-TWO

When I finally pulled up in front of Mrs. Staples's home, it was past the strict time she had set for our appointment, despite having left plenty of travel time.

As I sat there preparing myself for another tryst with Mrs. Staples, I detected the smell of Elliott's Bay Rum Cologne. Turning my head toward the passenger side I watched in fascination as Elliott suddenly appeared in my car.

All I could do was laugh.

"What is so damn funny?" he asked.

"When you do that you remind me of the characters in Star Trek when the captain would say, 'Hey, Scotty, beam me up.'"

"My dear, I can assure you we've been doing it longer and better than any Star Trek character," he said with a grin.

"Well while I have you with a smile on your face, I've got some bad news to tell you."

"What?" and the smile was gone.

"Well, you know how all the emphasis has been on the fact that you learned how to dance? Well, we might have forgotten one minor detail."

"What?"

"Elliott, I don't know how to dance. I've never danced slowly with anyone, let alone attempt to waltz with you." There, it was out!

For the longest time Elliott sat there quietly digesting the news. Digesting being a euphemism in this case.

"Well, I see we have a conundrum here, yes quite the conundrum."

"But there is a bright side to this."

"What?" Not a good sign, he was back with monosyllables.

"Mrs. S., my client, has offered to teach me to dance in just a few short lessons."

"Do you think she can? I mean, the waltz is a very complicated dance."

"Oh, she has assured me she can do it; she's had a lot of experience in this area," I lied.

Elliott looked somewhat relieved and I felt a tad bit better.

"However, I would feel better if we had an insurance policy here. I'm going to consult with the Masters. They may have a few tricks up their sleeves, too. Not that they have arms or sleeves for that matter," Elliott seemed very pleased with his new sense of humor.

I found no frivolity in it at all.

"Well, babe, got to go," and he began to fade out the same way he faded in. It was time for me to go too.

As I came up the porch stairs, I heard Mrs. Staples say, "Why are you always late?"

Not an auspicious beginning. I did what I usually do in this situation: defend myself.

"Just by a few minutes."

Where was she? She wasn't on the porch or in the garden . . .

"I'm right here."

Mrs. Staples was standing in the doorway of her home.

"So. Come in already."

My jaw dropped, followed quickly by a stomach flop.

"You want me to come into your home?"

"Of course! We don't want my neighbors to start talking."

"Talking about what?"

"Well, about the two grown women dancing on the porch."

"Dancing on the porch . . ."

"Of course, Regina. I am going to teach you how to dance. It is quite apparent that everything depends on your dancing with your husband, and dance you will!"

I know I heard what Mrs. Staples said, but for the longest time, her words did not register.

"You're going to teach me how to dance?" I asked, totally dumbfounded. For someone who was supposed to be a "sensitive" *a lot* of things seem to take me completely by surprise . . .

"Now, tell me. Did you ever take dancing lessons as a child?"

"No."

"But, Regina, everyone takes some lessons as a child. How did you prepare for your school cotillions?"

"My what?"

"Oh, heavens! Did you not go to your proms?"

"No."

"Why not?"

I didn't really want to tell her the truth. It was kinda embarrassing.

"No one ever asked me."

"Not a soul?"

"I guess I just wasn't the prom type!" I said defensively.

"Did you ever dance the fox trot or a slower dance, any kind of slower dance?"

Mrs. S. seemed like she was getting a little bit impatient, but there wasn't really anything I could do about that.

"Well, I danced at my first wedding but we mostly faked it. Elliott and I eloped, so dancing was never an issue."

"So, you have had some practice?"

"We took one lesson."

"Aha!" Mrs. Staples said triumphantly. "So you know how to stand and position yourself?"

"I think so." I strained my brain to recall one hour in the Arthur Murray Dance Studio many decades ago. I got myself into a ready position; that was the best I could really remember.

"My," Mrs. S. said, "we do have a lot to do before Sunday."

"What's Sunday?" I asked, trying not to let too much fear into my voice.

"Why, it's the summer solstice. And even though it's not on the goddess's feast day, neither your husband nor my daughter were anywhere near prepared to celebrate then, so now we must . . ."

Now I've always prided myself on being a fast learner, but I was really lost at this point in the conversation. And no matter how many times I had been lost lately, it had not yet become a feeling I enjoyed.

"Can you slow down and let me catch up?" I muttered. I needed to sit down.

"This is all about the Imbolc," Mrs. Staples said.

"What?! That's not helping!" I was practically yelling. "I'm getting really frustrated here, and that's not a good thing."

Mrs. Staples looked down at me and shook her head. "Don't talk to me about frustration, Regina. This has not been a lark in the park for me, either."

Mrs. S. motioned me inside and onto a wrought-iron seat in her entryway, then she sat down next to me. I could not help but feel a tad bit guilty. After all, she was just trying to help. I think.

"Look, Mrs. Staples. I'm sorry, but I'm lost with this whole goddess thing. All I want to do is learn to waltz and, excuse me, but get this goddamn thing over with."

"I understand, Regina, but first I must give you a brief history of the goddess. You simply must have this information, and I will try to give it to you as quickly as I know how.

"The feast day of the goddess Brigit falls every year on February first or second. It marks the first day of spring in the old country, and by that I mean Ireland, of course. It's a day of family reunions, of new life and wonderful dancing celebrations . . ."

As she continued to describe the meaning of this day, which I now understood to be called Imbolc, I began to look around the room. It wasn't that I wasn't interested; I just felt like I could Google all of this about the goddess later on my own, whereas taking in Mrs. Staples's environment was a one-time opportunity.

The room where we were sitting had the smell and pulse of an old fashioned parlor. Some of the furniture had been moved and a large rug had been turned up to show a beautiful wooden floor—presumably where we would be dancing. I had the sense that this room was never used and that nothing in it had changed in years.

I took the liberty of wandering around a bit while Mrs. S. was talking, not going so far that she would feel offended or realize I wasn't really listening. The parlor led out to a very formal dining room with all the places set with crystal and fine settings. I could not help but pick up one of the dishes and realized it was a very old Waterford pattern: hugely expensive and almost certainly irreplaceable. I put it down quickly but very gently.

I could hear Mrs. S. going on about the significance of the celebration, and I threw out a couple of "mmmhmms" to let her know I was still listening, but all the while my attention was fixed on a particular painting on the far wall. It was a watercolor done by the impressionist Charles Walter Stetson. It looked so familiar. I tried to ignore my impulse to take the painting down and examine the back of the frame.

I knew this frame, I really knew this frame. Another painting hung on the opposite wall, appearing to be a very old Bannister. Both artists were local to Rhode Island, and both had been very well-known to Elliott.

As I formulated a question for Mrs. Staples another painting caught my eye. Cows grazing in a field. Only Hayes painted cows like that. And once again, the frames were so familiar . . .

At that moment I realized Mrs. S. had stopped talking and was actually standing to my right.

"You appreciate my husband's art collection? There are many more in his gallery."

"Did he collect Rhode Island artists?"

"Not just Rhode Islanders, but New England artists in general."

"That's funny—so did my husband. He was an expert on New England impressionists."

"Take down the small Hayes and look at the back," Mrs. S. said.

And as sure as I lived and breathed, there was the gold tag with the Elliott Richards Gallery logo.

I looked up at her, and for a second I think I saw tears in her eyes. "We bought most of the art in this house from your husband, Regina. All bought and specifically framed in his shop!"

I was stunned and just a little angry. "So, you've known who I was from the start?"

"Not from the very first time we met, no."

"So when?"

"When Mr. Staples came to visit last May."

Did I hear that correctly? Her husband had visited her, too! I felt my mouth drop, and I could only gasp:

"That's why you believed me! You, too, have this, this . . ." I struggled to find the word. *Ability*," was what finally came out.

Mrs. Staples countered, "It's a gift. A gift, Regina. And my daughter has it, too!"

I was speechless. Mrs. S. pulled out one of the exquisite chairs from the dining room table, sat down, and motioned for me to do the same.

"Regina, I need to tell you my story, and please listen to me. You won't find much if you try and Google me!"

How the hell had she known about my Googling the goddess! Now she had my full attention.

"I was born in County Clare in Ireland. Even as a child, I knew I could see spirits. It was considered to be a great gift in the world in which I grew up, and I was always treated with great respect because of it. My family adored me, they treasured me, and my gift.

"We worshipped the goddess Brigit, and I knew all of the folklore surrounding her. The festival of Imbolc was steeped in ancient rites and prayer. As I've mentioned, it signified the beginning of spring. But now you can understand what an important time that was for those of us who live on the land. We planted our new fields and looked forward to the birthing of new livestock. Bonfires were lit throughout the countryside. When new candles were made and offered to the goddess, she in turn promised that the candles would last for the entire year. When yuletide greens were burnt and offered to her she saw to it that the coming planting season would be fruitful and pure.

"We would dance at midnight and visit with nearby family and neighbors. It was a very special time for my family and especially for me; I thought it would last forever. If only it could . . . Regina, are you listening to me?"

"Every word, ma'am. Every word."

"Good. Well my whole family wanted to stay on our farm forever, but it was not to be. The depression involved the whole world, and all over Ireland, farms were disappearing. Cultivating the land could not feed a family of eight. My da—that's my father, you know—left to work in the city, but he came back after several months when even the jobs in town had disappeared.

"Letters to America flew back and forth. Finally, one night, my mother made a very fine dinner. It was something we had not seen in a long time.

"After dinner, my father and mother began to speak to us about her uncle in America. He had left Ireland many years ago. He had since married and become a master loom setter in Rhode Island. His wife had died, and they were without children. Now he was offering my family passage to America. For this, we would live with him in his home. My mother would cook and clean, and my da would learn the loom trade. My uncle even offered to send the six of us to school in the parish, although he was dubious regarding the need to educate girls.

"It had been decided; just like that. The week before we were supposed to leave, my parents once again brought us together and explained that in the new country, devotion to the goddess was truly not accepted. They promised to always have a small gathering on her feast day, but anything grand was not to be. So the next night, we planned to have a great celebration—the biggest we ever observed! When I pointed out that Brigit's feast day was in February, not in June, my mother said that the day of the goddess could be any day, especially in America.

"My parents went to great lengths over the next two days to reassure us that the goddess would always be in our lives, but I don't think we believed them. My fears were confirmed the night before we were to leave when my ma and da sat me down to explain that my gift—my great treasure—would not be understood in America. They told me to embrace my gift and put it in a place in my heart where on occasion I could embrace it, but to never let anyone outside the family know the powers given to me by the goddess.

"As we climbed the gangplank to begin our journey, I did as instructed: I put my gift in a part of my heart that I would not see or feel for many, many years . . ."

CHAPTER TWENTY-THREE

I've always thought literary statements like "gazed in wonder" or "my heart raced" were totally overused in descriptive writing, but right now as Mrs. Staples looked out the window I could only gaze at her in wonder as my heart raced.

"Please tell me more."

"Oh, my," Mrs. Staples said. "I have not thought about this in such a long time . . . And now in the last six months, it's been all but consuming me."

Remembering my training with ladies of Mrs. Staples's age, I reverted to professional form and offered her a glass of water and a rest from our discussion.

She accepted the drink but not the rest.

On my way into the kitchen, I stopped in awe. It was huge. Uncannily deceptive from both the inside of the house and what I had gathered from the outside. Two full-sized sinks were positioned side by side, both constructed from a very fine-quality slate. There were two six-burner stoves with cabin-sized ovens and two industrial refrigerators, plus a freezer. The island in the middle of this culinary oasis was outfitted with additional burners for grilling and another small sink used just for prep work.

There were wine racks everywhere, and I could not help but stop to read some of the labels. Now, I am far from being a connoisseur, but I've had a glass or two of wine in my life. The bottles I regarded now were all of the ones I dreamed about purchasing for the most special of occasions. Beyond the wine collection, I viewed a sunroom that was smaller than the formal dining room but just as elegant. It overlooked the backyard, where my eyes traveled next.

What I saw there took my breath away. The entire yard was filled with plants, shrubs, and spring flowers. There were peonies and hydrangeas in all colors, with spectacular irises peeking their heads up everywhere. It was spectacular—so unlike the front of the house with those awful oak trees and drab, low hedgerows. The weeping cherry tree was by far the most beautiful specimen of its kind that I had ever seen. A small wrought-iron table and chairs invited me to dine here in splendor, too. Benches and marble figurines dotted the yard in a whimsical fashion, drawing my eyes—and my legs—further into the garden.

Stepping outside, I emerged from around a trellised set of vines to glimpse the center of the yard. There stood a large stone statue of a woman. Over five feet high, she was dressed in a rose-colored gown that actually looked like silk. Her shoes, which were more like slippers, were of the same rose color, and on each shoe was an unusual cross of gold. For a moment, I caught myself thinking: Really? Gold in the backyard?

Then I recognized the design as Brigit's Cross. Around her head was a crown bearing ancient letters inscribed in gold; the language was not one I had ever seen before, yet I could easily read: HEARTH, FIRE, AND POETRY.

Now how the hell did I know that?

I wanted to see the entire garden, inspect it inch by inch, and even lie down on one of the adjoining benches, but I heard my name calling me back to reality.

"Regina? Reginaaaaa?"

"Yes!"

"Where are you, dear? Are you bringing my water?"

"Yes!" I ducked back inside the house and saw her standing where she had advanced into the sunroom.

"I'm so, so sorry to be prying," I continued. "But it is so beautiful out here. How is it possible? I mean, all of the plants and flowers and shrubs are so extraordinary and . . . they coexist so magically? I mean, how can all of these different species be in full bloom together? I don't know a lot about gardening, but I know the weeping cherry is usually in bloom in late spring and the hydrangeas not until late summer . . ."

"It will all be explained in good time. But for now, please come back into the house."

"Okay, you go sit down, Mrs. Staples. I'll bring you your water."

I reentered the kitchen and hunted for a water glass. I somehow felt Mrs. S. would know the difference from a water glass and a juice glass.

Opening the nearest cabinet, I had to smile. Not only were the juice glasses separated from the water glasses by a clear and well-defined border, but all of the glassware was lined up with military precision. Stemmed wine gasses in a row. Unstemmed glasses as neat as neat could be.

Filling the glass, I hurried into the dining room and gave my hostess her water. "Who empties your dishwasher?"

Amazement filled her face.

"You want to know who empties my dishwasher? We are in crisis mode, and you want to know if I have domestic staff?"

"It's just that I have never seen glasses in a cabinet look like they are standing at attention."

For some reason I found this extremely funny and started to laugh, enjoying that laugh perhaps too heartily as a way to release some of my nervous energy.

"Please stop, Regina," Mrs. Staples asked me. "Please stop that now."

The look on her face brought me back to earth with a thud. Looking over at Mrs. Staples, I saw her age back in place. Her color was off, and her breathing was labored.

"I'm sorry . . ." I stammered into the silence. "I really am acting a little stupid here."

Mrs. Staples replied, "We have only a few days to make a miracle."

She continued, "All of the people involved have to know what is expected of them down to the last detail. If one aspect is out of alignment the consequences could be fatal."

That stopped me short.

"And I mean it: fatal! You and I have been handed a huge job. I am ready to take it on with my entire body and soul, but I need for you to be there with me."

Looking at Mrs. Staples, my mind played back all of the events from the past few months: meeting her, Elliott's whistling, music suddenly playing itself in the middle of the night . . . all of these things had led me here. To what end I didn't know. But I believed, for perhaps the first time, that I really needed to concentrate and follow her lead.

"I'm not going to say I'm sorry again," I began, "because to say it too often would diminish it and what I am feeling. So what I will say is that I am here to work and I want to work with you. I'm not sure why, but I will give you my all from now on."

"Thank you, Regina. I know you will."

The energy seemed to be returning to her face as she adjusted herself in her chair.

"Now where was I? Yes. I would not see my gift again for many, many years . . ."

CHAPTER TWENTY-FOUR

"We landed in Boston after a pretty uneventful journey. There was only one thing that made our trip unusual. In Ireland, most people were either farmers or city dwellers—both groups were poor, but neither really knew they were poor. We all basically ate the same food, wore similar clothes, and worshipped at the same church with the same religion.

"Onboard the ship as we sailed to our new home, I became aware of different ethnic groups for the first time. There were Poles and Italians and a few returning Americans. But we were all in steerage, so we were all poor.

"Then one afternoon, as I walked along the narrow corridors of the third-class hold, I spotted what seemed to be a clump of cloth in a darkened doorway. My initial response was to avoid it, but as I passed, the clump fell on its side, and to my great surprise I heard a sound emanate from it: 'Ma ma.' 'Ma ma.'

"I must have jumped up a foot. What made that sound?

"Frightened curiosity began to take over. I nudged the clump with my foot, but it was silent. So I nudged it again, but still nothing. The third time was the charm.

"'Ma ma!' The clump fell over again and landed on its front this time, revealing a part in the fabric of the material in which it was wrapped. I realized this object was vaguely familiar . . . it was a doll!

"But it was unlike any doll I had ever seen. I decided to get a better look at it, and peeled back the cloth to reveal a face with eyes, a mouth, and a nose—everything had been done in very fine detail, even the hands and two feet with fancy socks and wonderful, black, shiny shoes.

"I picked up the doll, and to my total amazement, the eyes closed! Her blue eyes disappeared, and she looked asleep in my arms. Of course, I had seen dolls before, but they were made of cloth or, more commonly, from pieces of rags. Maybe they had eyes made of buttons or a mouth made of ribbon . . . but I had never seen anything like this.

"Even the doll's clothes were layered. They started with a dress of a bright red color with lace on the hem and sleeves. Under that was a type of slip, as white as snow. It was stiff and made the dress stand out. Underneath that was a full set of undergarments made from lace with red bows, the color of the dress. I had never seen anyone dressed so finely—not even a new bride dressed in her wedding costume wore such fine attire. I had found a treasure!

"Then a thought jumped into my head and began to percolate. Maybe . . . just maybe . . . this was a gift from the goddess?

A gift to help me cope with the loss of my gift. After all, only the true goddess could have produced such a wonder.

"I thought I would take my find and go ask my mother. As I picked up my treasure, once again she wailed, 'Ma ma! Ma ma!'

"Next, I heard a voice cry out, 'Mother, I hear her! I hear Rose Catherine!'

"Now where was that voice coming from? It seemed as if it were coming from the sky. Was this another miracle?

"I decided I had enough heavenly intervention for one afternoon. Tucking the doll under my arm, I planned on hightailing it back down to our cabin.

"'MA MA! MA MA!' the doll persisted on crying.

"'Please be quiet!' I whispered to her. 'Please!'

"'Rose Catherine? Rose? Where are you?' the voice asked again from above. 'Mother, look, there she is! There is Rose Catherine! That little girl is running away with her. Stop, please stop! You have my doll . . .'

"Fear hit me in the gut, and I panicked. Down the stairs I ran two at a time. I must find my mother. Please, Brigit, help me find my mother . . .

"Turning to make sure I was not followed, I did not see the low beam. The next thing I knew, there was an explosion in my head—then blackness.

"I awoke several hours later. Although my head hurt, the hurt seemed far away. Gingerly, I sat up and looked around. Somehow I had landed behind a stone bench. The goddess's gift lay to my left, totally unhurt. I picked her up and slowly rose. Maybe this time I would walk to our cabin and find my mother.

"Opening the door, I was astounded to see da talking with two men in uniforms while Mother sat on the cot looking tired and nervous. They all turned to stare at me.

"Mother reacted first, 'Oh, El, are you all right? Where have you been?'

"Da was next, 'My little girl, we were so worried!'

"'Ma ma!' the doll cried out. 'Ma ma!'

"That stopped everything. A long silence met the cries.

"'Eleanor,' said mother in a gentle but firm manner. 'Where did you get the doll?'

"'I found her on the deck. Look at her! Have you never seen anything so splendid?'

"I noticed the glances between the officials.

"As da started to embrace me, one of the officials pushed him away and said: 'Little girl, did you steal this doll?'

"I was stunned. 'No! I found her on the deck.'

"The officer looked down at me and stated in a very stern voice: 'The little girl who owns this said you ran away with her doll.'

"'But I found her first and was bringing it to show my ma what the goddess gave me!'

"Confusion broke out and all parties were soon involved.

"My ma and da were not happy with my introduction of the goddess, and the officials were clearly uncomfortable with it, too.

"The other official now pounced: 'Where have you been all this time, hiding?'

"'No, I hit my head and must have lost track of the time.'

"'A very likely story,' he said directly into my face. 'Do you know what will happen to you and your family when you reach port?'

"'No . . .'

"'You will be put on the first ship back to Ireland!'

"My ma began to shake, and my da looked very sad.

"'I did not steal this doll! I found this doll, and I will not change my story, because I don't lie!'

"I am not sure what prompted me in that moment to have such a sense of self-possession, but everyone else in the cabin could only look at me. Next, there came a knock on the door, and another official called inside: 'An aside, sirs?'

"Our two officials left the cabin to confer. I glanced at my parents and said simply, 'If need be, I will return to the farm alone. I do not want to live in a place where I am believed to be a liar.'

"'Oh, El,' said my ma. 'You are just a little girl. Who will look after you?'

"'The goddess.'

"Both of my parents let out soft groans. Then the cabin door opened and one of the officials reentered.

"'I will take the doll, and consider this matter to be closed!'

"Confusion again filled the cabin.

"'What's happened? What's happened?' cried my da, but the official would neither answer him nor, for that matter, even look at us three.

"'Just be glad you won't have to go back to the Old Country.'

"With that, he grabbed the doll away from me and slammed the door, leaving us alone, scared, and totally at a loss for what just had happened.

"My da was furious. 'What, no explanation? No apology!'

"'Pat,' said my ma, 'Let it go. Just let it go.'

"He nodded to her, but in my heart I knew he would not let it go.

"Over the next few days, he asked around, as did some of the others in steerage who had heard the story.

"A few nights later, my da took my hand and strolled into the night. As we walked the deck we both became aware of the size of the moon. After we looked at it together for a long time, he turned to me and looked at me. His features were soft.

"'You are very young, El, but you are very brave. You were very brave the other day . . . We know you would never steal that doll. The little girl who owns the doll lost her, and rather than tell her parents the truth, she lied and said the doll was stolen.'

"'Why? Why would anyone do that?'

"My da didn't answer, so I continued. 'And why would they think I would lie, but she could not?'

"He took a sharp, deep breath. 'Life can be very unfair, El. You will learn that as you grow . . . There will always be those who think they are better than us, just because they have the good fortune to be better educated, or because they have more money than we do. But remember this, and believe it in your heart. We will always be on the side of the goddess Brigit and be better for it!'

"I looked at my da that night and loved him as much as a girl can love her father. But nonetheless, something had died in me that night I was called a liar. I decided at that very minute that if I ever had the chance to pick between the goddess and education, social standing, and money, the goddess Brigit would lose, and lose hands down."

CHAPTER TWENTY-FIVE

Here, Mrs. Staples stopped. I glanced over and willed her to go on. I simply couldn't imagine not getting to hear the rest of the story today. I know it sounds selfish, but as Mrs. S. herself said, time was of the essence!

"Would you like some more water?" I asked sweetly.

"No, I just need a minute, please."

"Maybe we should finish this another day?" I asked, with the tone of voice of someone who really didn't want that to be the case.

"No, I'll be fine. Where did I leave off?"

"You and your family had just entered the United States."

"Yes. Yes, well, life became very predictable then. Predictable if you could predict that our great-uncle would be such a bad man.

"Mother took control of the house: cooking, cleaning, laundry . . . Just about anything and everything our great-uncle could think of. One particular summer, the mill went on strike, and with no income coming in to the household, our great-uncle decided we were going to plant a garden. And not just any garden, but one with every vegetable imaginable: potatoes, carrots, cucumbers, lettuce, and a whole bunch of other things I had never heard of. Because gardening was 'a lady's chore,' he dumped the entire task on my mother. He even expected her to till the soil!

"Our great-uncle forbid my father from helping and sent him off to look for work—even though to approach the shuttered mills would put my da's health in peril from the strikers. We kids would watch our father leave in the early morning, not knowing what shape he might be in when he returned. My ma continued to do all of her usual daily chores and then go out to the garden to do her 'fun' chores.

"But, you know, Regina, I always felt our great-uncle thought mother was just too slow in the garden . . . almost as if she was being tardy on purpose . . . It was only with great reluctance that he finally allowed my father to help her, which allowed the two of them to be together for at least part of every day.

"Our great-uncle resented everything—he even resented sending me and my sisters to the parish school, even though it was free. But what really upset my parents was when my oldest brother was offered a full scholarship to the private, Catholic, all-boys school and our great-uncle opposed it. That was the first time my mother and father began to talk about leaving and going out on their own.

"Well, that really frightened the old man. He dropped his opposition, but he made one demand: no monies marked for the household could go toward my brother's uniform, transportation, or other sundries. My brother alone had to earn that money."

Here, Mrs. S. paused again, and this time, I let her rest. I thought over everything she had told me. It was quite a tale, and certainly one that had shaped her, from the doll story to calling her parents "mother and father" instead of "ma and da." Finances and education had taken on a great significance, even at a very young age.

I was beginning to feel I had learned enough for one day, and that I could actually come home reasonably satisfied, when she interrupted my thoughts.

"If you would be so kind, Regina, would you please pour me a sherry?"

"What?!"

"You heard me." She pointed to an ornate wooden cabinet that stood just inside the door to the parlor. The sherry was the color of liquid gold, stored in a beautiful hand-blown carafe.

"And please have some yourself."

"No, I think I'll pass . . . I'm driving, you know."

That earned a look from Ms. S. that proved her spirits were strong enough to continue. I poured myself a small glass.

As I sat there sipping my sherry, my thoughts began to wander. I knew this story was related to the overall plan, but I really had come here today to learn how to dance.

Mrs. Staples continued, "In 1960, our great-uncle died."

That locked my attention back in. I wasn't expecting that.

"Was it sudden, or . . . ?"

"Oh, no! That would have been too easy. He suffered a series of strokes, each one of which made him weaker and more difficult to deal with. Finally, he was confined to his bed, and my parents were totally responsible for his care.

"This burden fell almost entirely on my mother. Of course, we children were growing and had taken on more of the household chores, but it was my mother who dealt with the screaming and the ranting. I don't think any of us will ever forget the sound of bedpans hitting floors or the yelling that would suddenly stop or the sound of slapping taking its toll . . .

"My father tried to intervene, but my mother would simply say, 'Pat, he doesn't know what he's doing. Mostly he misses me, anyway.'

"When he finally passed, a wake was held. We invited all of his friends, but no one came. The next day, at his funeral, some people came, but they were mainly friends of my parents. It wasn't until later—after, as my father said, he was planted—that people showed up. But they didn't come to offer condolences. They came to eat and drink and sing and dance. Their show of grief lasted into the next day . . .

"And it was that next day that our great-uncle's attorney made it to the house to read the last will and testament. We dressed in our best but prepared for the worst. My father was overheard telling my mother, 'He would probably rather leave everything to a band of gypsies than see us get anything.'

To which my mother replied, 'Oh, Pat, how much could he have anyway,' adding in a whisper, 'If only he would leave us the house or somewhere else to live . . .'

"Twenty minutes later, we sat in stunned silence. Not only had our wonderful, saintly, and generous great-uncle left the house to my parents, he had also left them a great deal of money, all in something called a trust. And he had left each of the children trusts, too! A little more for my brothers, but certainly enough money for the girls to begin to think seriously about educating ourselves. And not just high school but college, too. Our lives were turned around in minutes.

"It was only many years later that I came to the conclusion that my family had really worked for that money. Especially my ma."

I noticed that Mrs. S. had finished her glass of sherry.

"Want another pop? I mean, would you like another drink?"

"Maybe just wet the bottom of the glass. And would you pour for yourself as well? I really don't like to drink alone."

Fetching her glass, I noted how cool her hands were, almost cold. "Can I get you something to eat? It must be close to your dinner time."

"I always eat at seven thirty, so I am hours away from dinner."

I glanced at my watch. Not yet 5:15.

Mrs. Staples looked at me and said, "Can I get you something to eat? It must be close to *your* dinner time."

I glanced over to see if there were any humor lines on her face. There were not.

Lying, I said, "I had a big lunch."

"Then let us continue.

"As you can imagine, our lives changed dramatically. Father continued to work at the mill but was promoted to master loom setter, our great-uncle's former position. Mother hired a live-in housekeeper and had a young man from the town come in weekly to do the heavier chores, such as beating the rugs, chopping wood, and doing the lawn maintenance—all of those things which had been the sole responsibility of my parents.

"My older brothers went off to high school and college; my older sisters married into good families and began to set up their own households. My own childhood slipped away, and before I knew it, the image of myself in the mirror as a young lass had been replaced by that of a young lady.

"In high school, I wanted to study everything, and not a month went by that I did not change my intended vocation. One month, I wanted to be a pediatrician; one month, I wanted to be an archaeologist. I dreamed of writing a wildly famous novel that would later be adapted for Broadway and be produced to rave reviews.

"Owing to my indecisiveness regarding my career track, my parents tried to dissuade me from attending college right away and offered me the next best thing: travel. Along with my mother, I did the 'grand tour' of London, Paris, and beyond. We took in all the finest museums, dined in only the best restaurants, and housed ourselves in five-star hotels. With each piece of clothing purchased from the finest houses in Europe, I prayed that our trip would never end, but alas, it had to.

"We were on our way back to America onboard a ship approximately the size of the one that had first carried our family from Ireland—except now we were lodged in a first-class cabin. On our third day at sea, I decided to take a walk before dinner. I was honing my list of the things I needed to share with my father, the real highlights of the trip, when I heard a sound that stopped me in my tracks.

"'Ma ma! Ma ma!' I ran to where the sound was coming from. There in a deck chair sat a beautiful child, a little girl of about four years old holding a porcelain doll so similar to that doll that had been the cause of so much consternation those many years ago. But what really fascinated me was the girl's loving face as she gazed up at a young man. They appeared together as a unit, and I felt I was interrupting a sacred interaction.

"Just then, the young man looked up at me and smiled. I froze. As our eyes met, it seemed that my heart both raced and stopped at the same time. It was the first time I saw Frank. Mr. Francis Thomas Xavier Staples III.

"Once again, my life as I knew it ended on a ship in the middle of the sea."

I had never heard a story that swept through so many years as if all of the events were unfolding right before my eyes. There was nowhere I would rather be.

"Frank was twenty-three years old that year, traveling with his mother and his much younger sister. They were returning from Ireland, where they had been to spend time with his mother's parents.

"My return trip took on a whole new agenda. We walked the deck as often as we could. Sometimes his sister was with us and, to my delight, sometimes she wasn't. We had so much to talk about that we never lacked for topics of conversation. If something new or surprising happened during my day on the ship, I would think, *I can't wait to tell Frank*. We were so filled with each other that we didn't even notice the troubled looks between our mothers and their hidden whispers.

"As we neared Boston and ultimately Providence, we made plans to continue our discussions. We lived on opposite ends of the city, but there was public transportation. Frank would finish his internship in July of the next year and was planning to open up his own medical practice in the city. I would finish my last months of high school in January, and any thoughts of college were gone from my world. We felt the fates had aligned themselves to bring us to each other and that we were poised to grow up and old together.

"Perhaps we should have been more cognizant of those glances between our mothers. Maybe then we would have been ready for what happened next.

"On a very hot and humid Sunday in August, my mother informed me we were going to tea with friends. Just the three of us. A little out of the ordinary, but not unheard of. Yet I was filled with dread when my father pulled up to the Staples's home on the East Side of Providence.

"Entering the home, we were greeted by Dr. Staples and his wife. Frank joined us shortly thereafter; one look on his face, and I began to fear that no good was to come from this encounter.

"The older Dr. Staples jumped in immediately. Both set of parents had met several times and were all in agreement. They were not happy about our plans. There were many reasons. I was too young to even consider a life with Frank. He was just starting out and would need all of his time and energy to devote to his new practice. Frank's trusts had been largely used for his education, and his major source of income was not to mature for three years. My trust, although much smaller, would be mine upon my eighteenth birthday, but this was money that had long been reserved for me to earn a college degree.

"I remember crying out, 'I don't even want to go to college now! I want to be with Frank!'

"'Quiet, girl!' stormed my father. 'You don't even know what that means!'

"It was clear the meeting was over, and we were dismissed. My anger was so intense toward my parents that at first I started to resist their calls for our departure. One look at my father's face silenced me from expressing myself in his direction, but my feelings continued to overwhelm me, so I aimed my anger at the only person in the room with no more authority than me: Frank.

"Hours later, sitting alone in my room, I rolled over all the hurtful things I had said to him and felt very sad. All night long, my words came back to haunt me as I shifted from anger to depression. In my mind the blame shifted from my parents to him and then back to me.

"By dawn, I knew what I had to do. I would write Frank a letter, a letter explaining the reasons for my outburst. A long letter begging him for forgiveness. After an hour of intense writing—all of which wound up on the floor—I had an inspiration, one so grand and so right I thought for the first time in a very long time of the goddess Brigit. Was it she who had put this idea into my heart?

"Off I went to make the trek to the oak-lined streets of the East Side. An hour later, as I headed up the driveway, I spotted Frank's car. I raced to the driver's side and placed the envelope under the windshield wiper. Making sure it was secured, I started down to the street, when, to my horror, I spotted Frank coming toward me. Changing my direction, I headed for the backyard.

"I had a perfect view of his car and watched with excitement and fear as Frank noticed the envelope and reached for it.

"As he read the note I had that special heartbeat, the one that is both a rush and a stop. What happened next fills me with love for this man to this day. A smile as big as a full moon came over his face, and I knew all was forgiven, that somehow everything was going to be all right.

"And it was all because of a note I penned to Frank. And it had simply said, 'I'm sorry.'"

CHAPTER TWENTY-SIX

"We ran away when I turned eighteen. Frank had a tiny practice, and we had my trust, but most of all, we had each other. We loved and respected one another. We created our own world and had no desire to let anyone else in, never felt the need—until the unthinkable happened. Something we never saw coming. I got pregnant!

"Paula Ann Staples was born a Pisces. Initially, I felt some love for the tiny little girl in front of me, but as I looked into my husband's eyes and saw the transition of his love ebb from me to her, even that slight love began to fade. By her first birthday, it became clear to me my feelings had evolved from mild appreciation into a dark sense of dislike. I will not say hate, never hate.

"Regina, you see, I just didn't like my daughter. Once again, my life had taken on a new dimension, except this time without the sea and without the ship.

"People always told Frank that he and Paula had a special bond. They shared everything, whether it was high culture: a love of the classics, for example, or religious music and ceremony, or popular culture such as ice hockey. They spent hours pre- and post-game dissecting the local hockey team, while I hated hockey. To this day I hate hockey.

"Regina, I can honestly say that the family and friends who were in our lives, who watched as Paula grew, watched me, too. No one ever would say to me, to my face, what they felt in their hearts, but it was there. They all firmly believed I had no ties to my daughter. And they were sure I never would. And they were right!

"But I did watch her closely to see if she had inherited the gift. I watched her when we spoke of loved ones close to death, I watched her the first time she attended a wake and funeral, and she showed no capacity for it. None at all. And I never mentioned the gift to her either, not even once. I even allowed myself a period of relief when I was certain she had no ability to talk to or see the dead.

"But, of course, I was wrong. So very wrong . . ." Here, she stopped briefly, and a long, tired sigh escaped her lips. I had to remember that she was a lady of a certain age.

Suddenly, Mrs. Staples looked up and smiled, "Regina, where was I?"

"You were telling me how sure you were that Paula was free from inheriting your abilities. Which I think was setting me up for you turning out to be wrong."

Mrs. S. smiled a slightly irked smile.

"Ah, yes. Paula had just turned twelve. Our elderly neighbor, Mrs. Johnson, who had been ill for a long time, had died. The neighborhood rallied around her family as they struggled;

their grief was different, having had a long time to prepare, but it was in no way easier.

"Paula was nowhere to be found during our preparations. As we cooked and baked and readied for the wake and funeral, she remained uninvolved. Because this was the first time she had had to deal with the death of a nonfamily member, I was not overly concerned. It was only after several days had passed that I decided to ask her what was wrong.

"Because conversations were rare between my daughter and me, I was not surprised when I sat next to her and she opened with 'Now you want to talk? Now it's time?' Her anger was so forceful it slapped at my face.

"'Do you know how afraid I was?' she asked me. 'How horrified when it happened?'

"My heart felt cold as I asked, 'What happened? What frightened you?' Not wanting to hear the answer, of course . . .

"'When I saw Mrs. Johnson standing in the garden right after she had passed! She spoke to me. She told me I was the first one she had shown herself to because I had the gift. You see, Mother, it never occurred to this spirit that I would not know I could see and hear spirits. After all, what kind of mother wouldn't tell their daughter of the great treasure she may have inherited? What kind of mother would not prepare their daughter and protect them from the shock of seeing spirits for the very first time? This kind of mother, one with no heart'—here she was pointing directly at me—'I had to learn about my gift from a ghost. I'm done with you, Mother. I don't know what I ever did to you, but right now, I don't care. I'm really done, and I'm done with him, too,' she said, gesturing toward the house. 'Anyone who can stay married to you for all these years is not human either.'

"'Paula,' I begged, 'please do not bring your father into this. He is not even aware of any of this. Please don't hurt him because of me.'

"But by then, Paula had left the garden. She never addressed the issue of the gift again, or any other issue at all for that matter. Not her first car, nor her first love, nor her choice of college and career.

"She mellowed with Frank and let him into her world at times, but that unique bond between them was gone. Frank never talked about it, but I knew he was hurt. We simply returned to our own nest, our own world, and saw fewer and fewer people, until by the end, our only real visitor was your husband, Elliott, when he came to sell us some paintings."

I really wondered, would now be a good chance to segue into the dance lessons I had come for? I couldn't really imagine breaking this dear lady's train of thought, but what if this apocalyptic series of events *did* go down this weekend and I was not prepared?

Mercifully, Mrs. Staples read my mind.

"Well, Regina, I think the time has come to stop this dialogue for now."

I couldn't help but think, *Interesting use of the word "dialogue . . ."*

"What music are you familiar with? And please, nothing written after the year 2010?"

From the corner of the living room, Mrs. S. wheeled out a record player. Yep, a real, live, hi-fi record player. This lady kept on surprising me.

"Wow, how old is that monster?"

"It is not a monster. Her name is Cassandra, and a lady never tells her age." Having said that, I swear she giggled.

"You named your record player?"

"Actually, Francis did. He had a wonderful gift for naming things he loved, and some of the people he nicknamed were very grateful . . ."

Mrs. S. looked into the distance wistfully, and I was afraid this might lead us into another longish tale of her husband or family life.

"What do you have for music?" I asked.

"Well, many things. Classical, folk music from the old world, some popular music . . ."

"We need to find a waltz."

"Well, for that we might want to look at the show tunes. Now, what kind of a waltz are you looking for? Viennese style or American style?"

"Hell, I don't know."

"Well, let's see what we have . . . *The Sound of Music* has a waltz."

"I hate *The Sound of Music*."

"*South Pacific?*"

"Yuck."

"How about *Finian's Rainbow?*"

"Let's hear that . . ."

Mrs. Staples placed the LP on the turntable as if handling a precious gift. We listened to the music for a few minutes until a totally rejuvenated Mrs. Staples could not help but grab my hand and lead me to the impromptu dance floor.

It would be so easy to say that with the magic of the music and the knowledge of our quest, I was lifted off the floor in a miracle and mastered the waltz!

I did not. I did not feel the music, and my feet remained solidly planted on her living-room floor.

We tried for an hour. No amount of one-two-three, one-two-three inspired me to actually dance. My steps were more like a plod, a very sad plod.

After several attempts in vain, I simply sat down on the floor and started to cry.

"Regina, that is not going to help," Mrs. S. admonished me. "Please stop. We need to rethink our plan."

Here my cries turned to sobs. "I can't do this! I've let everyone down. You'll never see your daughter, and Elliott may be relegated to a zoo . . . This is hopeless!" I continued to sob.

"It is not!" Mrs. S. said firmly with a flash of her iron will. "We simply must rethink the plan."

Suddenly, out of the corner of my eye, I detected a faint movement in the garden and then the smell of the Bay Rum cologne.

"Oh my God, I think Elliott is here," I whispered to Mrs. S. "I think he's in the garden. I smell his cologne!"

She sat as still as a statue. "I think, no I do . . . I smell the cologne, too!" she hissed.

I picked myself off the floor and ran out into the backyard.

In the midst of the hydrangeas sat my husband, looking very sad.

"What are you doing here? How did you know where I was?"

"Oh, babe, I always know where you are."

"Ohhhhkay. Did you get to consult with your Master?"

"Well, I did let him know we have a problem, but he's stumped, too. The fact is, no one saw this coming."

"So, now what?" I was trying not to let my hysteria shine through.

"Well, he is off consulting his guides."

"So what do we do in the meantime?"

"I guess we just wait for their guidance."

As we sat mulling over our dilemma, I noticed Elliott looking over to the house with interest.

"I know this house. I have been here many times."

"Yes, you have," I hastened to explain. "This is Mrs. S.'s house. She and her husband were clients of yours. You sold them some great pieces. They have a nice Bannister, and a Stetson in the living room, and a gallery you helped set up."

"What's their last name? You only referred to her as Mrs. S."

"Well I have to keep client privilege, you know."

Elliott chuckled. "Regina, I'm dead. Who am I going to tell?"

"Well, you have a point there . . . Dr. and Mrs. Francis Thomas Xavier Staples III."

"Frank and Eleanor?"

"Do you remember them?"

"Of course! Wonderful folks, so knowledgeable and gracious."

An idea crossed my mind and made me smile for the first time in the last several hours. "Hey, do you want to come in and say hello?"

"I would love to, but I cannot. I simply cannot just go in and say hello."

"Why not?"

"I need to be invited in. Those are the rules."

"Well, I never invited you in . . ."

"To paraphrase someone I love, *Duh!* I owned our home."

"Oh, right . . ."

So deep in conversation were we that we never saw Mrs. Staples come into the garden.

"Hello, Elliott," she said.

We both jumped a foot.

Astonished, I shrieked, "You can see him!"

"Oh, Regina, really! Of course I can see him. You know we share the gift."

"Indeed! I must have forgotten. It's been a pretty long day."

As always Elliott, even a dead Elliott, was gracious and respectful to the opposite sex. "How are you? You are looking well."

God, was Mrs. S. blushing?

"How is Frank?" Elliott asked. "Is he still a visitor?"

"Sometimes, not very often," Mrs. S. said wistfully. "I think he is ready to move on, but he needs us to resolve this first."

"Yes, we do seem to have a dilemma on our hands," muttered Elliott.

Mrs. Staples seemed to perk up again. "Please forgive me, Elliott. Would you like to come into my home?"

"Why, yes, I would!"

Upon entering the home Elliott seemed to glide from room to room and from painting to painting. "You haven't changed a thing, have you?"

"No, you and Frank had such a perfect eye for placing everything. I haven't even been tempted to move one single painting."

In the meantime, I was trying to wrap my mind around the happenings of the last twenty minutes. My late husband shows up at my client's home and realizes we actually share the client. Meanwhile, the client who can see my husband, invites him into her home. And once inside my husband inspects his handiwork of thirty years ago. It was a lot to absorb.

Suddenly, Elliott grew pale and looked almost, well, for a lack of the correct adjective, dead. Very dead!

"Sorry, got to go. I think the Masters need me now . . . Wait here, and I'll try to return very soon."

And then he was gone. My emotions went all over the place—from sadness to curiosity to hope and to dread. It was at least five minutes before I could look up at Mrs. S.

"Do you think we could have one more drink?"

Twenty minutes later, we were sipping the last of our glasses of a very, very good port.

"How long should I wait here?" I asked Mrs. S., forgetting for a moment that she was of our world, not theirs. "Do they even have time over there? I need to feed my cat and—"

The aroma of Elliott's cologne permeated the room again.

And he was back. He looked wonderful with his glowing skin and infectious smile. "Good news!" he announced. "The Masters have found a solution."

"My dear," he gazed at me, "we will be dancing after all." Then turning toward Mrs. Staples he said, "Paula is on her way home. Our dreams will all come true. Regina, you will learn to dance tomorrow, and we will waltz on Sunday."

"But how? I am hopeless!"

"My Masters studied the entire problem and all of the different facets. They looked into past lives and past planes and realized one of the most successful ballroom dancers in the world is presently living within walking distance of this very house.

"She has agreed to bring her magic to help us out. She is going to bring her secrets of the hummingbirds to us. The hummingbirds are going to instruct you in the dance."

"That's a grand way of saying it, Elliott."

He acknowledged my compliment with a slight bow. "And my sweet, sweet Regina, you know this fine lady."

"I do? Who?"

"Her name is Dr. Piffs? Dr. Roberta Piffs. Regina? Regina, what's wrong, you look sick . . ."

CHAPTER TWENTY-SEVEN

The bile that hit the back of my throat was akin to the Titanic hitting the iceberg.

"Are you nuts? Piffs? Piffs!"

Both Elliott and Mrs. S. stared as I slowly sank to the floor and crawled into a fetal position.

"No no no no no no nooooooooooooo . . ."

Sometimes in life, I feel like what I need, despite my tough exterior, is a gentle hand and compassion from my fellow travelers. Instead, I got:

"Oh, Regina, grow up!" from Elliott.

"Stop your whining," from Mrs. S.

Elliott tried logic on me next. "The Masters have produced the tools and we need to use them."

"But Elliott, can't you try to find someone else? Can't the Masters resurrect Ginger Rogers or something?"

"No!" they bellowed in unison.

"Dr. Piffs has agreed and is on her way," Elliott said.

And with that the front doorbell rang.

Mrs. Staples practically leaped at the door.

This left a moment for Elliott and me to be alone.

"Oh, God. Please let me just wake up from this nightmare . . . I just want to go back to a time and place when dancing shoes and dancing spirits were things only in my head . . . And to a time before that, when they weren't in my head . . ."

Elliott knelt down and took my hand. "Regina. Please, Regina, you have to understand what is happening here. You must see the bigger picture."

"We are all involved, but so are you. You have something to gain, too."

"What?"

"Your book. You will now be able to write your book. Everything that has happened and is about to happen will make a great memoir of our lives together. It will be the first chapter, the starting point of your huge success. It is about to change your world.

"You are not just a conduit for all of *our* hopes and dreams. You are the reason this is going down. We are doing this for you."

Slowly, once again, the reality hit me. That strange calmness that hit an hour ago was coming back.

"This is all about me writing a book, a tale not just of our love, but of bigger issues?"

"Reincarnation and past-life issues, forgiveness and trust and finding your lost life plans. Put them all in your book."

And now let's say hello to Dr. Piffs and welcome her and her hummingbirds.

CHAPTER TWENTY-EIGHT

Dr. Roberta Piffs stood in Mrs. Staples's foyer, appearing cool and calm. "Hello, Regina."

"Hello, Dr. Piffs," I said weakly.

"I suppose you should call me Roberta. After all, I expect we shall all be sharing a journey together soon. And please introduce me to your friends."

It was the plural form of the word that really struck me. "Friends?"

"Well, I can see two of them."

Mercifully, Mrs. Staples came to my rescue. "I am E. Staples, and this is Regina's late husband, Elliott Richards."

"Very nice to meet you, sir. I have heard so many nice things about you."

"As I've heard about you, also," Elliott stated in his most polite voice.

Now where was that coming from? 'Cause I'm thinking if he's heard nice things about her it hasn't been from me!

Hmmm, I thought. *Do ghosts lie? I guess they could, but then again, would their lie be a sin? But they're dead, so would a sin count against their soul?*

"Hello! . . . Regina?" Elliott said, waving his hand in front of my face. "We need you to keep focused."

"Oh, I'm focused. I'm as focused as you can get. After all, I'm addressing a ghost, and a ghost that everyone here can see! So you betcha I'm focused."

Here, Elliott felt compelled to address the group, "Please forgive my wife. She tends to prattle on when she gets tired."

As my three companions stared at me, I could feel all of the tension from the last few days boil to the surface. I could practically smell the tension. But one look at Elliott made me channel it all back down.

He looked so sad and uncertain. Just like all the times when he was alive and knew we were heading for a discussion on some topic. A discussion known to the rest of the world as a screaming, shrieking, fist-shaking fight. I knew I had to let it go.

"Well, to tell you the truth, I am tired. This has been a long goddamn day. I say we discuss a plan for tomorrow, set an agenda, and call it a night."

Mrs. Staples concurred, "It is almost eight o'clock, and I'm in need of some nourishment and sleep."

"I need to feed the cat," I muttered.

From Roberta: "I have some ideas for the music we will need, so I need to go to my office and pick up some CDs."

Did she just wink at me?!

And from Elliott: "I don't need sleep or food, no longer have a cat and"—nodding to the doctor—"I will leave the choice of music in your capable hands, but I could use a little time away on a nearby plane to collect my thoughts for tomorrow."

After the day we had, I was almost afraid to drive home, and it didn't have anything to do with the alcohol. My mind was completely alert, but every bone in my body that had attempted to dance was now in revolt.

Maggie greeted me at the door and made a point of letting me know that I needed to feed her ASAP and that her litter box needed attention, too. While opening her can of food it hit me that I hadn't eaten today either. Even the cat food smelled appetizing.

Opening the refrigerator I pulled out two slices of pizza that could have been as old as the last century. But they tasted good! Ah, the miracle of chemicals.

And speaking of chemicals, I decided to tackle the litter box. It resembled some of the nuclear debris that had floated over to the west coast of the U.S. from Japan after the tsunami.

"Hey, Maggs? You sure you're not throwing orgies in here when I'm out?"

Her look was one of pure revulsion. What kind of orgies does a seventeen-year-old cat have? And excuse me, with whom?

Mind you, all this in a six-second communication bullet.

"Well, I'm off to bed."

I trundled off, clearly expecting to fall asleep and stay asleep through the night. But at exactly two A.M., I woke up as if a bomb had exploded outside the bedroom.

"Jesus, I still can't dance," I repeated over and over to myself. It became my mantra of horror. "Suppose I can't learn to waltz or even almost learn? Suppose—"

"I have all the faith in the world in the eminent doctor," Elliott said from across the room.

"Holy shit! Where did you come from?" I gasped. "Don't do that! Are you trying to kill me?"

"Sorry. Sometimes I forget that I'm dead."

"What? How can you forget that you're dead?"

"Well, it's not like you have a sign on you saying ALIVE and I have one that says DEAD. I'm in my own home in my bed talking with my wife as I did for more than thirty years, so I guess I just forget that I'm dead."

"Well, just look down and see what you are wearing. That will bring you back to reality," I said, pointing at his tux and dancing shoes.

The laughter that burst from us was deep, and it felt damn good. Maggie jumped up on the bed and stared at me and into the space where Elliott was hovering.

Then she turned on herself and fell into a purring heap in her usual space that she occupied every evening when we were still a family of three.

"This is so cool," I said.

"What is?"

"Having you back again, even if it's not for a long time." I chose my words carefully as I continued. "I think it should be looked at as a type of lottery prize."

Elliott looked up quizzically.

"I think if a couple really loves one another and respects one another and is kind to each other while they live then that couple should be awarded a chance to spend time with each other when one of them passes."

Looking at Elliott I really felt a need to tell him something I never told him when he was alive.

"I thank you for my life with you. You are the reason I'm me. My confidence and my strengths are all because of you. And now I want to thank you for thinking of me in your death, and I really am happy you are back to dance with me.

"And I know everything will work out tomorrow and Sunday."

"Regina, you can be such a nut sometimes," Elliott said. He continued, "All of you, all of what makes up Regina Richards was in place when I met you. It just needed to be tweaked a bit."

"I thank you for that anyway. You sleeping here tonight?" I asked.

"Yes, I think for a bit."

"Then you need to take off your dancing shoes."

"Okay. Good night, babe."

"Good night, Elliott."

"'Night, Miss Maggs," we said in unison.

CHAPTER TWENTY-NINE

The next thing I was aware of, the morning sun was coming into my room. I had no idea of the time but surmised a problem when the phone started to ring.

"Good morning, Regina. It's Roberta."

"What time is it?" I shouted into the telephone.

"Relax, it's only seven o'clock. But I wanted to give you a wake-up call just in case you accidentally slept in."

Always on the defensive with this woman I said, "Why would I?"

"Well, Elliott did tell me you and he had a pretty late evening, and I don't want to add to Mrs. Staples's anxiety level if you were late again. "Regina, are you there?"

I felt my anger level begin to rise as I digested what Dr. Piffs had just said. Why were all my buds comfortable sharing this information with her?

"Regina, please don't go there," Piffs said, as if she could read my mind. "We really don't have time for this today."

Now I was fuming!

"I'm sorry. What is it that you don't have time for today, Doctor?" I retorted in my best staying-calm-but-ready-to-blow voice.

"Please drop the defensiveness. Everyone knows you have a history of tardiness. Regina, you know it drives Carol to distraction. So let that go."

With a hop out of bed I said, "Okie dokie, my lateness is no longer an issue. And you know what I'm going to do, Roberta?"

I could feel her anxiety building. "Oh, Lord. What?"

"I'm going to forget you even said anything about my so-called late night with my deceased husband."

"I am totally amazed," she gushed. "And so very pleased."

"You know what else, Roberta? I'm going to get out of bed, take a shower, eat my breakfast, feed my cat, get in my car, and drive into Providence. I'll see you at eight thirty with my dancing shoes on. My happy dancing shoes, my happy, happy . . ."

"Enough, Regina, I get it. You are turning over a new leaf, a mature leaf, a leaf you . . ."

"Oh, no, Roberta, I have the floor! Otherwise, this 'who can be more uplifting' pissing contest could last all day!"

Laughter broke out across the great divide.

"See you at eight thirty," Dr. Piffs said.

Walking into the bathroom, it suddenly surfaced that I had laughed with Dr. Roberta Piffs for the very first time.

And it felt good.

Maybe today would be a good day after all.

* * *

Two hours later, and that good feeling was disappearing fast.

"Regina, please listen to me. You need to relax," Roberta said.

"I am relaxed!" I could see Roberta biting back a comeback.

"I need more coffee," she said.

"Me, too," I said but was immediately met with a resounding "NO!" from my gal pals.

Mrs. Staples sat in her wing-back chair and glanced over at me with troubled eyes. "Regina, have you ever danced in your life?"

"Well, of course . . . but I can't get this waltz thing. It doesn't play in my head."

Looking at me again she said, "Maybe it needs to play somewhere else?"

"Such as?"

"Your ears and then continue on down to your feet." I couldn't help but notice that the gleam that had appeared in Mrs. S.'s eyes when we started up this morning was gone now, replaced by an almost apathetic gaze. I was really disappointing her, and I didn't know what to do about it.

When Roberta returned, she rolled back the Persian rug to expose more of the floor.

To this activity, I said, "Maybe if I have more room to dance, I'll learn faster!"

"No, that won't work," said Roberta, completely missing my sarcastic bent.

"Well then, where is this hummingbird magic you so assured us could help me learn to dance?"

"I only want to use that if we get desperate."

"Oh, we're not desperate yet. Let's take stock of the situation. It's after ten in the morning. It's Saturday and Elliott and I are scheduled to dance sometime tomorrow afternoon. But let's not get desperate, because any minute now we're going to be gliding around the room like Fred and Ginger.

"Jesus, Roberta! Elliott is so anxious he can't even stay in the house. He's been sitting in the garden wondering what it's like to be a kangaroo or maybe a hippo. But is he desperate? Noooo. And poor Mrs. Staples, well, she—"

"I think I can speak for myself, Regina."

Mrs. S. stood up from her chair, and I was taken by her regal pose, all signs of apathy gone. "I have full faith in you, Regina, and in you, Roberta. I am not desperate. You two must simply figure things out together without my interference."

She went to join Elliott in the garden.

Roberta admonished me. "You need to realize that Mrs. Staples is well into her eighties and she needs to be cared for, too."

"Are you kidding me? That lady is as strong as a horse. I don't want to be in the same room or house or, for that matter, block when you tell her she needs to be taken care of."

"I bow to your expertise."

"Yeah, right."

"Regina," Piffs began reflectively, "How long have you been working with elders?"

"Too long!" I retorted defensively.

"Really, come on. How long?"

"Almost eighteen years."

"Wow! Did you ever want to do anything else?"

"Yes and no. It was never part of the master plan to do this work, but I knew I was hooked after I met my first self-neglecting ninety-year-old."

"What were her issues?"

"His issues. He was a local artist that everyone thought was batty. He lived in a pit over on the other side of Doyle. No heat except from an old fireplace and electricity jerry-rigged from a neighbor's home."

Memories flooded back to me. The house was so overgrown with weeds most people didn't even know it was there. The client had appeared at his door dressed in cut-off jeans and a sweatshirt on a cold, snowy, January day.

"The neighbor paid for his electricity?" Roberta said, pulling me back into the conversation.

"Too scared of him not to."

"And you weren't scared of him?"

"Leery, at first, definitely. Until I saw his art. He was a genius; he had painted with the big boys all over the world. His stories were mesmeric. He could remember conversations he had with Picasso in Paris during the war verbatim but couldn't remember to eat daily."

"Why were you there to see him?"

"Someone called city hall to report that an old man was living in a dangerous situation, and when city hall looked him up, they found he had not paid taxes in years."

"So what was the state's priority, his safety or the back taxes?"

This brought on a giggle. "Well, it depends on whose perspective we're talking about!"

"What happened to him?"

"We got the city to back off the case and let him stay in his home for about two years. Elliott even orchestrated a showing of his work at the gallery. Now that was a show. Some people are still talking about it. And then, in the blizzard of 2000, his roof collapsed, trapping him inside. He died in the only place he ever loved."

God, I had not thought of him in years.

"What happened to his paintings?"

"A cousin from Michigan showed up and took them back with him. Don't really know what happened to them."

"He took them all?"

"Well, not all . . . There was a little bartering going on between him and Elliott to pay for the gallery showing."

"Do you have some pieces?"

"Maybe yes, maybe no." God, why couldn't I drop my attitude once and for all with this woman?

"Well if it's maybe yes, I would love to see them."

"Maybe yes, maybe no," I decided to stick with the attitude for old time's sake.

"You know, Regina, when you talk about your clients, you glow and really relax."

"Yeah! They're like my own somehow."

"Elliott must have been very proud of your work."

"Oh, no, no, not at first. After I graduated with my masters degree in social work, he wanted me to have a nice office with secretarial staff and fifty-minute hours and four-day work weeks. You know, something very clinical and professional. You should have been around for the weekend when we entertained a group of Elliott's swanky New York clients at a very famous restaurant in Providence. While we were dining out on the veranda, my client Edward, who was seventy-four and homeless, clambered over the railings and tried to hit me up for ten bucks. He put on a real show. It wasn't pretty, and Elliott was *not* amused . . ."

Suddenly, Roberta jumped up from her chair and began to pace the living room floor. Back and forth she strode doing her best interpretation of a caged lioness. You could almost see wheels turning in her head and the air being exchanged inside her lungs. I was impressed.

As suddenly as she had started to pace, she now stopped. "Regina, I got it! I think I have an idea of how we are going to beat this."

"How?"

"I think we just forget about waltzing for now. We need to concentrate on getting you to relax and feel the music. You said yourself you weren't feeling the tempo—"

"Yes, that's true but—"

She pointed to the middle of the floor. "I want you to sit right here. Picture this as a beautiful and grand ballroom. You are surrounded by your self-neglecting clients that have passed on. Some you helped, some you didn't, some of them made you laugh, and some of them made you cry. Talk to them! Welcome them, tell them you are so happy they are with you and will be a part of the great miracle that is going to happen here."

"But, Roberta, I can't just conjure up people."

"Not people, *memories* of people. Memories of your clients. Just like you did a minute ago with the artist."

"But to what purpose?"

"So they can relax you. You are so calm and filled with confidence—even joy—when you speak about them. We are going to surround you with this antistress potion. And when you feel relaxed, your feet will meet your head, and your body will join in, and this room of memories will begin to sway and move and—do I dare say it—dance!

"Now I'm going to get the other CD I want from my car. While I'm gone, I want you to begin to talk to your clients as if they were right here."

"You want me to talk to them out loud!?"

"Of course."

"What do I say?"

"Well, now, how would I know," she said with a little smirk. "They're your clients. And you're always telling us you're the expert regarding your clients . . ."

When she left the room, my mind was as jumbled as ever, but what the hell—nothing else was working, so . . . Here goes.

"Who wants to be first?" I said to the ceiling. "Step right up! Anyone game?"

I'll never really know what happened next. But suddenly I had the biggest green and red hummingbird in my face, darting all around me. Up close and personal. He was followed by a smaller female, who actually sat on my shoulder for a second.

They spun around the room, and as they did, they made low chirping noises. And I knew the chirping was for me. *Go for it, girl! You can do it!*

Bring those memories into the room, now!

All time stopped as I spanned the room: good clients, some bad clients, but all dead clients began to materialize.

They were all talking at once—some to me, some to others—but all were talking. I spotted Leo and Pearl. Hastening to their side, I took her hand and said, "God, Pearl, it is so cool to see you again. I'm so sorry I never went to your funeral, but your lawyer never told me you died. And Leo, are you still walking?"

"I manage a few miles a day."

To my artist friend, Herbert, I said: "I still have the paintings, you know. I never sold any."

To which he replied, "Well, hang on to them, my dear. I hear through the grapevine that my cousin is doing quite well marketing them. You may have a little nest egg there for yourself one day. And how's Elliott?"

"Dead. But he is here today."

I didn't know when statements like that would stop sounding strange, nor did I know when responses like Herbert's would stop sounding strange either: "I'll have to look him up."

As I moved from client to client I was totally unaware of anything else. The entire living room had come alive.

Out of the corner of my eye, I saw Mrs. Staples standing in the doorway watching me with a look of amazement.

"Elliott, please, come here, dear!"

As Elliott came into the room, he looked at what was going on in the room with a look of great trepidation.

"Elliott," Mrs. S. whispered. "Does she do this often?"

Elliott whispered back, "*No!* I've never seen this kind of behavior before."

What they were seeing, or in this case not seeing, was me running around the dining room laughing and making hugging and hand-shaking gestures. Bending down and making patting motions in the air.

"She looks awfully happy," said Mrs. S. "Elliott, dear. Do you think we may have pushed her too far? Maybe she's lost it?"

Roberta reentered the home and watched with a huge smile on her face. Tears streamed down her face.

"She really did this. And she did it for us."

"What's she done?" asked Mrs. Staples.

"She has found a way to relax, to forget her fears of dancing, so now we can move on."

Mrs. Staples stammered, "This is Regina . . . unstressed? She is running around the room talking to the air. There is no one here!"

Roberta started to laugh. "Oh, relax, you two—everything is going to be fine!"

"Regina!" Roberta called. "Regina, come here a moment."

I dashed over, not wanting to lose a moment of time with my clients.

"I'm afraid you are scaring these two."

"Why?!"

"Because these are your memories—we can't see them. You need to let us see your memories."

"Oh, sure."

Suddenly, the dining room was filled with people, much to the relief of Elliott and Mrs. Staples.

"Elliott: Herbert is here, and Leo and Pearl—"

"So is that homeless person, I see—"

"He's not homeless anymore!"

"Hmmph!"

Roberta stepped in to take charge. "Okay, everyone! This reunion is great, but this is not why we're here. We have a lot to do and very limited time. So let's get started."

Leading Elliott and Mrs. Staples to the perimeter of the room, Roberta continued to address the group. "Okay. Our mission is to get your friend and case manager, Regina, to dance. She will then dance with Elliott, her husband, who, in turn, will then see his way toward brokering a truce between your hostess Mrs. Staples and her daughter, The Reverend Paula Staples. As for me, I have no agenda here."

To which I thought, *Bullshit!*

"This CD is by the artist Christo"—here a few murmurs of approval broke in—"So let's go. Let's dance!"

The music filled the room. It began slowly and started to reach its height. But no one moved.

Suddenly, the room was filled with hummingbirds, hundreds of them. They danced to the music. Up and over they danced in pairs, they danced by themselves, female with male, male with male. It was as if a well-choreographed ballet was being performed in front of us.

And suddenly, I felt it. It began as a tapping in one toe, then two, then it spread through my foot and leg and all at once I was dancing.

And I wanted everyone to dance. Grabbing Herbert, we did a jig, and he went on to dance with Leo; I paired Pearl with the non-homeless person, and they glided on by. Mrs. S. sat in her winged chair clapping to the music.

Roberta appeared out of nowhere and the Mexican hat dance was danced as it had never been danced before. Everyone was dancing!

And when the music stopped I knew in my heart I could and always would be ready to dance with Elliott.

* * *

Much later that night, as we lay in our bed together going over every inch of the day, we held hands, after a fashion. Maggie lay in her usual spot.

"Are you ready for tomorrow?" he asked.

"Yup. What should I wear?"

"I wouldn't worry about that—I've had that covered for weeks."

"You always were the planner," I said. "So tomorrow we dance—and then you're off?"

"Yes."

"Will I ever see you again?"

"You won't need to. You'll be moving on to bigger and better things than me."

"Never, babe. No one will ever be better."

"Maybe better was the wrong word. I should have said different. But I will make you a promise: I'll keep checking in on you. And if there comes a time when you need some comfort and care, I'll always be close. After all, death does not have to be so permanent."

I confess I had to think about that one.

"Thank you."

"You're welcome."

Suddenly, Elliott chuckled. "Those hummingbirds were awesome. Who gets to dance with hummingbirds?"

I agreed. "Yeah. Who else spent the day today learning to dance from hummingbirds?"

CHAPTER THIRTY

The next morning, I woke up to the sound of rain pounding on the windows and thunder in the distance. Rolling over, I gloried in the notion that it was Sunday and I could stay in bed. *I don't care if it rains all day,* I thought, *I'm not going to leave the house.*

Oh, shit, it's Sunday! This Sunday!

Scrambling out of the bed I hit the floor and made it to the window in three seconds.

"Maggie! Maggie, it's pouring out. It's not supposed to rain today!"

Looking rather uninterested, Maggie glanced over and yawned her best morning yawn, signifying, at best, only a kernel of concern.

"How come I never saw this coming?" I said out loud as I ran over to the computer to check the weather. I couldn't remember the last time I sat here . . . As a matter of fact, I couldn't remember the last thing I did that was not related to dancing. Had I eaten, and when? Had I showered, and when?

I remembered at some point feeding the cat and cleaning out the litter box. But when I did that was a mystery.

The weather report did not make me happy. Showers and cool temperatures seemed destined to fill the day.

"Elliott! Hey, Elliott! Where are you?!"

"Here, I'm here! What's wrong?"

"Babe, it's wet and stormy out. Can't you do something about the weather?"

"Like what?"

"Make it sunny and warm."

"Regina, I can't. And I don't think it will matter what the weather is—we'll be indoors anyway."

"Are you sure?"

"Yes, dear. Why don't you eat a nice, healthy breakfast, and I'll brush down my shoes. Again. I guess I'm pretty nervous, too . . ."

We puttered around the house for a little while. I did the dishes and fed the cat, making sure she had enough for several days; I'm not really sure why. Before I headed into the shower, I asked Elliott, "Since you've been dead, have you met anyone you might find interesting? I mean interesting like me?"

"No, Regina. I think you have spoiled me in that department for a long time. I may not ever find someone as interesting as you!"

An hour later as we prepared to leave, the home phone rang. I looked at it and debated whether to allow this intrusion into my, no, *our* day. But I picked it up anyway.

"Hello?"

"Hi, Regina. It's me, Carol."

Not so threatening, only Carol.

"What's up?"

"I just had an interesting call."

"From?"

"From Piffs's husband."

"Really?"

"He says he hasn't seen her for two days."

"Does he sound worried?"

"No . . . more curious than worried."

"Why did he call you? Doesn't she have friends he should contact first?"

"No, he seemed to think that you and I were her only friends."

"Interesting. Well, if I see her I'll tell her to call home. Got to go!"

"Got to go?! No interesting insight into her disappearance?"

"Nope! She'll turn up."

As I headed for the car, I rolled Carol's news over in my head. *Hmmmm, no agenda, you say, Dr. Piffs? Well, we'll see about that, won't we?*

My thoughts were interrupted by Elliott as we drove toward the city.

"You do not know how to drive, babe."

"You never complained about it when you were alive. Now it bothers you?"

"I never drove with you when I was alive. I always drove."

"Just sit back and relax. What are you afraid of, a fatal accident or something?" I started laughing and laughed for a long while before I realized I was laughing by myself.

"Just keep your eyes on the road."

"If my driving is so bad, why don't you just fly there or do whatever you usually do?"

The silence that filled the space was dark. It reminded me of the time several years ago when we were waiting for the results of his biopsy. We knew the truth, but until it was official, there was still always hope.

I knew what was going through his mind, then as now. We only had a few precious moments together, but if no one said it out loud, maybe by some kind of miracle the time could be extended.

So we continued to make our way to Providence in silence.

As I turned down Mrs. Staples's street I was taken by the sight of a limousine parked in front of her home. Not the traditional black funeral vehicle, but a compact shiny mini-limousine that oozed class and, dare I say, money.

I turned to speak with Elliott, but my car was empty. Where did he go?

Walking toward the house, I was again struck by the two different yards. There was the almost barren front and the lush, Eden-like garden in the rear. The parallel between the yards and their owner was startling. Mrs. Staples's façade was stoic and even cold. But inside that body were a heart and soul that were trying hard to be warm and inviting.

The door was opened by the good doctor.

"Good morning, Regina. Isn't this exciting! The day is finally here!"

"Not to be a killjoy or anything, but you do remember that I have yet to dance a waltz?"

"After yesterday, I am not worried at all. You'll be fine . . . Now, come in and meet Paula. She is very lovely. Did you know she is an ordained Episcopal bishop?"

"Big deal."

"What do you mean, big deal? It is a big deal! Regina, really, how could you be cranky today, of all days?"

For some reason, when someone challenges my lack of enthusiasm, I always have the desire to bring them down rather than to try to rise to the occasion. And suddenly I knew how I could do it.

"Got a call from Carol this morning. Said she got a call from your husband? He hasn't heard from you in two days. So he called the only person he associates as a friend to ask about you. Carol said he did not seem overly concerned, more like mildly curious as to your whereabouts?"

I was imagining the eminent doctor reacting as I had hoped. Dreams smashed. All semblance of elation gone. Thoroughly depressed and worn.

Wrong! A big smile erupted on her face and, dare I say it, she seemed to dance a little jig.

"Oh, no, lady. You are not doing that to me today! If that dickhead really wanted to know where I was, why would he wait two days to look for me? He is not going to bring me down, and you certainly are not going to either. No, you need to check your attitude at the door. Do a little soul searching before we go any further."

Boom! Now who was feeling depressed and worn? I decided it was not the time to meet the bishop and went out to look for Elliott instead.

I found him in the front yard gazing up at the oak trees.

"I'm not a big fan of oak trees," he said. "But Frank loved it out here. Much more than the backyard. He felt the oak symbolized independence, while the backyard was all but given over to St. Brigit. And he was not really a fan of the goddess. Always believed she was the start of the rift between mother and daughter."

"Elliott, he was right. The chief reason for their lack of communication had everything to do with the goddess."

"Well, so how am I supposed to make peace between them when I know nothing about their relationship failures."

"I think you will just be a sort of conduit here, a pass-through, if you will. I think the goddess is going to be doing all the work."

"Well, that is a relief!"

I told him what had just happened between Roberta and myself.

"What is wrong with me?" I asked. "I really wanted to hurt her."

"No, you didn't."

"Yeah, I did."

"No, you didn't."

"Yes, I did!"

"Reggie, the person—for lack of another word—you really want to hurt is me."

I looked over at him and once again felt the volcano in my heart erupt, but as quickly as it started to boil over, it was gone.

"You are right. I guess part of me still can't quite handle that you are dead."

"That is why you need to move on and get on with the book. I know I've said it a lot, but this book will be your passage out of here. It will bring you into another world. But there are even more pressing reasons for you to write it. The world is ready for it!

"You have always been destined to do great in this world, and this book will only be the start of a movement that will give the world one more shot at fixing itself. And, Regina, it may be the last shot it has.

"So, now, let's go in and meet Paula and help her mend her relationship with her mother. And then we will dance. I will hold you, and we can pretend we are anywhere in the world, or we can be right here in Mrs. Staples's living room. And we will look at each other and our souls will once again touch just as they did so many years ago at the Art Club on our first night together.

"Do you remember that look? Do you remember how your heart raced and your mind turned? It will happen again tonight, I promise you. We will fall in love again tonight.

"But, Regina, when the dance is over, then you need to move on with your life and your book and your love. One day, hopefully soon, you will enter a room and look over to the other side, and your heart will race, and your mind will spin, and your gaze will lock on another, and your spirits will touch again. Let it happen, Regina. Find your soulmate again. And who knows, my love, maybe if we are really lucky, it could even be me."

CHAPTER THIRTY-ONE

As I entered Mrs. Staples's living room, I became aware of a feeling pulsing in my head. I was having a great deal of difficulty naming that feeling, besides the fact that it felt weird. And it would not go away. Then it hit me; it was shyness. I was feeling shy! I could not for the life of me remember the last time I felt shy. Public speaking classes in grad school?

Wow!

"Hey, Elliott," I shouted out, "I'm feeling shy."

He materialized in front of me and quickly said, "Reggie, you don't have a shy bone in that skinny body."

"Why is this happening? Why am I feeling this now?"

"Could it be you are anxious to meet Mrs. Staples's daughter? She is a very well-known scholar and an ordained bishop, you know."

"It must be that . . ."

"I thought it was no big deal a few minutes ago," said Roberta, walking out of the dining room.

"Always the last word. Can't let it go without your input. Piffs, sometimes you make me so mad, no wrong word, *so fucking mad* I could . . ."

"You could do what," she said, as she started to walk toward me.

Elliott made an appearance just in the proverbial nick of time and somehow planted himself between us.

"Reg, Reg, let it go."

"No, Elliott," Piffs said. "I want to know what exactly she would like to do. We have been having this conversation for almost five years, and I still don't have a clue as to what it is she would really like to do."

The silence was deafening.

I could see Elliott in front of me, his eyes pleading me, begging me to just let it go.

"You know, Piffs, what I really want to do to you? I mean, really, really want to do?"

I heard a soft moan escape from Elliott.

"I want to come over and plant a big, fat kiss on your forehead and tell you I checked my attitude at the door and gave myself an attitude adjustment and just want peace."

It was then I realized my newly reacquainted sense of shyness was a precursor to my new less angry self. When I walked through the door today I had been reborn. How it happened, why it happened, I couldn't say. But it felt good.

At that moment, I realized both Roberta and Elliott were staring at me.

"Babe, what just happened?" Elliott asked. "You're just about glowing!"

"Elliott, I think I'm ready to move on. No. No, I *know* I'm ready. Thank you, Roberta. Thank you.

"I know why you are here. Only you, only you could bring out these feelings of disgust and dislike. All of this time I've known you, I've felt repulsed by you, and now I know why.

"I've been jealous of you, jealous of your education and your degrees, your social status, and yet without you here I could not have finished my rebirth. I needed to really hate you to grow."

"Thank you," the doctor muttered. "I think . . ."

"No. Thank *you*."

Turning to Elliott, I simply said, "It's time."

As the three of us entered the dining room, we all caught sight of Mrs. Staples and her daughter sitting at the grand table. To say Mrs. Staples looked radiant was an understatement of huge proportion. Mother and daughter sat close to one another, their hands firmly clasped in each other's. The tears had all been wiped away, and they sat almost in their own world listening to each other and talking to each other, truly enjoying each other for the very first time.

I turned to Elliott and said, "I think the goddess Brigit has already been here and accomplished her miracle. Your job with them is done."

Elliott looked up and said, "Well, I am very relieved that part is over. Now what about your part, are you nervous?"

"Nope. The old Regina would be quaking in her shoes with the idea of waltzing with you, but the new Regina is ready to get this done."

"Yay!" said Roberta.

As if by magic, the lights in the dining room dimmed, and the floor seemed to heave slightly. The walls were filled with candles and stars, and wonderful smells filled the room. Hydrangeas, peonies, and tulips were everywhere.

My jeans were gone, replaced by a dress of the finest cream-colored silk.

And we were no longer in Mrs. Staples's dining room but in the Art Club. The Art Club where we met and fell in love. The very place our souls had touched the first time.

I whispered to my husband as we stood taking in all the changes, "Did you arrange all of this?"

"It was my idea, but I needed some help! You look very beautiful, more beautiful than the first time I saw you."

"And look at you, so debonair and worldly in your tuxedo and your dancing shoes."

The music began vey quietly and very slowly. We walked to the middle of the room and began to dance.

Gracefully, artfully, we danced. Just like Fred and Ginger. Probably not. But for the two of us it was the most thrilling, most incredible, and most private five minutes of our time together.

And when it was over, it was just that: over.

We knew what came next. But sadness was not going to be part of it, not now.

Just the joy of what we had and the knowledge that what was possible could always happen again.

There would always be hope.

"Hey, Elliott, just one more thing. Do you think you could find a way to leave those dancing shoes behind? Maggie has taken quite a shine to them."

THE END

ACKNOWLEDGEMENTS

I have always wanted to write our love story. None of this would ever have happened if it was not for my late husband Erwin W. Deines. Without his pure love, patience, and humor, my life would have been empty.

I owe much to Lisa Tener, my Book Coach, who inspired me to keep on writing. And to the women in my writing class who were the very first souls to hear a little of *Hummingbirds*. Their feedback made my dream come true.

I can't thank my editor enough. From our first meeting, Stuart Horwitz "got it." My message was loud and clear in my mind, but it was a dream. Stu was able to make it a reality.

And to all of my friends and colleagues who encouraged me to keep on writing. Armine Donabedian, Barbara Curran, Tedd Lodi, Linnea Tuttle. Thank you will never be enough.

To family who urged me to get my story told, Linda Feldman, Paula Marinaro, and especially to my sister, Barbara Reardon. Thanks.

Finally, I need to thank the one person who was there almost at the beginning of my journey. I need to thank my best friend, Joanne Campbell. She encouraged me to share our love story and never doubted I would finish my task.

ABOUT THE AUTHOR

Photo: Kristin Elliott

A Dance with Hummingbirds is Helen Deines's first novel. Having spent over twenty-five years working with the elderly, she has since retired and lives near Providence, Rhode Island.

CPSIA information can be obtained at www.ICGtesting.com
Printed in the USA
BVOW08s2048240715

410097BV00002B/81/P